Wild Ride

D0827262

Wild Ride

Jacqueline Guest

James Lorimer & Company Ltd., Publishers
Toronto

© 2005 Jacqueline Guest

James Lorimer & Company Ltd. acknowledges the support of the Ontario Arts Council. We acknowledge the support of the Government of Canada through the Book Publishing Industry Development Program (BPIDP) for our publishing activities. We acknowledge the support of the Canada Council for the Arts for our publishing program. We acknowledge the support of the Government of Ontario through the Ontario Media Development Corporation's Ontario Book Initiative.

The Canada Council | Le Conseil des Arts
for the Arts | du Canada

ONTARIO ARTS COUNCIL
CONSEIL DES ARTS DE L'ONTARIO

Cover design: Clarke MacDonald

Canada Cataloguing in Publication Data

Guest, Jacqueline
   Wild ride / Jacqueline Guest.

(SideStreets)
ISBN 10 1-55028-880-6—ISBN 13 978-1-55028-880-3 (pbk.)
ISBN 10 1-55028-881-4—ISBN 13 978-1-55028-881-0 (bound)

1. Métis—Juvenile fiction. I. Title.

PS8563.U365W54 2005   jC813'.54   C2005-900262-X

James Lorimer & Company
Ltd., Publishers
317 Adelaide St West, Suite 1002
Toronto, Ontario
M5V 1P9
www.lorimer.ca
Printed and bound in Canada

Distributed in the
United States by:
Orca Book Publishers
P.O. Box 468
Custer, WA USA
98240-0468

For Ron,
the greatest son-in-law in the world
and a treasured friend.

The author would like to thank Constable Kathryn J. Goodyear, RCMP National Summer Student Co-ordinator 'K' Division Recruiting Services and David Volk, Computer Wizard and technical advisor for their expert advice in the writing of this book.

Chapter 1

January Fournier stared at the stretch of treacherously winding mountain road ahead … and smiled.

This was going to be fun. Gearing down her red and white Yamaha YZR 600F motorcycle, she started into the corners. As bike and rider leaned hard over in the first turn, Jan knew that her knee was only millimetres above the pavement. It was like a sixth sense with her. She accelerated out of the corner, easing the bike to vertical as she picked her best racing line through the next tight turn, then roared into it.

Her bike handled like a dream. She flew through the corners, leaning her machine from side to side like a choreographed ballet as she blasted down the twisting highway. She was on her way to school, but there was always time for a fast ride — emphasis on the *fast*.

She'd successfully handled her last corner and was setting up for the next when she caught a flash of black up ahead. Reflexes instantly took over. Jan stepped on the back brake pedal with her right foot as her gloved hands pulled in the clutch and firmly squeezed the brake lever. Simultaneously, she banged down through the gears with her left foot. The bike shuddered to an abrupt stop. Her heart thumped hard against her chest as the adrenaline ramped up in her bloodstream.

Barely ten metres ahead of her on the highway, a large black bear rumbled out of the bushes at the side of the road and started across the exact spot she would have been had she not stopped. Immediately behind it, two smaller bundles of black tumbled out of the underbrush and scampered after their mother. Jan knew that encountering a sow with her cubs is always dangerous and possibly deadly, but this time the mother ignored the rider and her motorcyle and worked on getting her boisterous babies across the road instead.

The cubs looked so comical and clownish, Jan had to smile at their traffic-stopping parade. Flipping her visor open, she breathed in the crystal-clear mountain air. The late April sunshine dazzled her eyes as it reflected with diamond brightness off the scattered snow patches. Despite the unexpected excitement around any bend in the road, this had to be the coolest commute any kid in Canada could have!

Once the furry family had safely crossed the highway, January blipped the throttle, tapped her visor shut, and continued to school. Life was sweet.

* * *

It was Friday, so Jan had to get through only one more gruelling class before the weekend. The problem was that the last class was computers, not her favourite subject. Reluctantly, she slid into her seat and wished she felt better about the new assignment. She and a partner were to design and build a web site — complete with graphics, sound, and animation — that dealt with a topic relevant to the Banff National Park or their school, Banff Community High.

The part that worried Jan was that this project would make up fifty per cent of her final grade. So far, she wasn't exactly passing computer class with flying colours, and she knew if she didn't get a great mark on this project she'd fail the course.

Jan would attend the University of Calgary in the fall and wanted to end her high-school career on a high note. She would be taking a B.A. in Law and Society and, by going year-round, would finish in three years, not four. Then, if all the planets aligned as she hoped, she'd continue on to law school in Victoria. A career in the law had started as her dream years ago, and now she was determined to make her dream come true. Her friends said she'd need tons of good luck to pull it off, but Jan knew that luck had nothing to do with it. To her, good luck was simply a special brew made up of careful planning, hard work, and gallons of sweat.

She pushed her short black hair behind her ears.

Wearing a motorcycle helmet every day did little to help her hair, but she didn't care. It wasn't like she had anyone to look great for.

"Okay, people, everyone sit with your project partner and let's get started," Mr. Volk, their computer teacher, instructed. With a lot of scraping and shuffling of chairs, the students rearranged themselves, pairing up in front of computer terminals.

Jan looked around. She didn't have a partner and was acutely aware of the other students' curious stares. She'd been a senior here for a month and still felt like an outsider. The girls in her class weren't overly friendly and she wondered if it was because of the way she looked, which, she had to admit, was different from every other girl in the room. They wore their hair in the latest styles, used tons of makeup, and dressed in really hot clothes. At seventeen, Jan was a slim 5'8" and did none of the above, which made her somewhat of a freak with her peers and meant there wasn't exactly a lineup to have lunch with her. Being a loner didn't bother her, but she thought it would be nice to have help building this dumb web site. She stared at the dark screen and wondered where to begin.

"Do you have a teammate, or can I have this seat?" a deep voice asked as a backpack was unceremoniously dropped into the chair beside Jan.

Jan looked up into a smiling face partially hidden behind a pair of expensive-looking sunglasses. She frowned. She didn't like pushy guys and avoided them like the plague. Josh, an old boyfriend, had been bad news and, ever since he'd seriously jerked her around, the male half of the species wasn't on her radar. "Ah, no — I mean yes," she answered lamely. "I mean *no* I don't have a partner and *yes* I do mind." She scanned the room, hoping there was another girl who needed a last-minute partner, but she could see she was on her own and had no choice. "But since we're the last two left in the room, I guess you're the winner by default." Jan shoved the guy's backpack unceremoniously onto the floor.

Lowering his designer shades halfway down his nose, he wiggled his eyebrows at her. "Great! It's so nice to be wanted. B. Liam Simpson, computer wizard, at your service." He swung his leg over the now-empty chair and booted up the computer.

"I'm January Fournier. But before we team up, I have to warn you, I don't know the difference between a CPU and a CP-me. Being my partner could be hazardous to your final grade." She felt it only fair to warn this over-eager computer geek. As she waited for B. Liam Simpson to start back-pedalling, she studied his face. She took in the summer-sky blue eyes and the honey-coloured hair. He was a little on the lean side — maybe skinny would be a better word — but that was okay, as bulging Neanderthal muscles did nothing for her. "What's the *B* stand for?"

"*Better-not-ask,*" he answered casually as he flexed his fingers until they cracked.

Jan cringed. She'd always hated that particular habit.

"If we're done with the formalities, Miss Fournier, it's time for you to stand back and prepare to be dazzled, because computers and I get along really well. I write wicked script. Our web site will rock. Now, let's make some magic!" He pushed his sunglasses up onto his head. "Don't worry about being a rookie. It's actually a good thing — no bad habits to unlearn." His fingers flew over the keyboard.

Jan couldn't believe this guy's ego. "Gee, thanks. What a nice thing to say." She didn't try to hide the sarcasm in her voice but, watching him work, she had to admit he seemed to know his stuff.

"Write this path down," he instructed, reciting a long list of letters and symbols. "We have to document all the steps we take. Then, if there's a problem, we can see where we detonated. Also, Herr Professor Volk really likes to see every drop of sweat we pump in." He continued talking as he worked at warp speed. "We'll have to write some code, but that shouldn't slow us down. I'll get started building us an empty framework." Text blinked and colours flashed across the computer screen.

"Uh … shouldn't we decide on the topic first?" Jan asked, irritated with the way her new partner had waltzed in and taken over.

Liam shrugged. "It's not necessary right now. We can hang stuff off the template later." As he shot Jan a look, he must have seen the fire in her eyes, because he stopped typing. "Okay, what super cutting-edge issue do you want our web site to be about?"

Jan pursed her lips. "Actually, I haven't a clue. We're already light years ahead of where I thought I'd be." She knew this was due to Liam's obvious talents, but wouldn't tell him that. "However … since this is a team project, we should both agree on the main idea. That way no one will feel forced into something or left out." She waited for him to see her logic.

Liam's eyes slid back to the screen. Jan could tell he was totally focused on it, not her. "No problem. I'm on board with whatever you come up with. You tell me what you want and how it should look. I'll have a world of cyber-monkeys blasting through the Net to our site in no time." When Jan didn't say anything, Liam flicked another glance at her. "If that's okay with you, that is. I don't mean to be pushy, but sometimes I get a little carried away."

"I guess it goes with being a guy." Jan opened her notebook with a snap. "Hormones or something. Liam, I'm serious. We — as in *both of us* — have to choose a topic before you get too far into this."

"Fine. We'll do it your way," Liam agreed, not reacting to her slight. He furrowed his brow; his pale brows drawing together in what Jan called a *frinkle*, a hybrid between a frown and a wrinkle. "I think something to do with how the new computer lab has affected the students here would be appropriate. It was a huge shift from old to new technology. We could do a spreadsheet with a typical grade point average before and after access to the world of search engines, then interview students about possible careers as techies. Hey, we could have a page on computer games! I know megabytes about gaming."

Jan held up her hand. "Wait a minute. This should be something related to the outside world. The computer lab is a lame topic. How about something with a little more human interest? Hey, what about the Banff Springs snails? The park is the only place in the entire world they're found. We'd explain how the park is trying to save the unique species by protecting their habitat. We could have a presentation charting the life cycle. Maybe do a slide show of the original cave and basin where the snails were first found."

He gave her a look that screamed, *Get serious*. "Snails, huh? Gee, that really grabs my attention."

Jan's mouth took on a hard line. "And computers is any better?"

They glared at each other, then Liam relented.

"Look, we can come back to a topic later. I have to build a basic web page to put the information on anyway. Let me do that while we're getting to where we can agree on something." Before Jan could say anything, he went back to typing in commands.

Jan slumped in her chair, resigned and resentful. Maybe it would be better to give this more thought. They were going to work long hours on the project, and she didn't want to rush into anything they weren't both excited about. "Okay," was all she said as she reluctantly capitulated.

Jan watched Liam work for a couple of minutes. He never stopped the frantic pace. His fingers looked possessed, moving at light speed, until he finally sat back with a satisfied look on his face.

"Done." He smiled and saved his work to a tiny USB flash drive that he slipped into his pocket. Reaching into his backpack, he pulled out a notebook with a cover made of old printed circuits, opened it, and scribbled a line of symbols. "I've seen you around once or twice. You new to Banff?" he asked without looking up.

She thought about telling him that it was none of his business. Then she realized they might have gotten off on the wrong foot, and she didn't have to be snotty to the guy. He was probably just making polite conversation. "Yeah, my family moved here late in March, when my new stepdad graduated from his RCMP training in Regina and was posted to Banff," Jan explained.

"You're from Saskatchewan?" he asked.

"Nope." Jan shook her head. "We're originally from Bragg Creek. It's only an hour and a bit away, which practically makes us locals."

Liam nodded. "I know Bragg Creek — nice little town. I've never been there personally, but I've seen the web site."

Jan looked at him in surprise. "You visited the web site but not the town?"

"Yeah. It's not as messy when you e-travel. No problems with schedules, passports, lost luggage."

"But aren't you missing out on a lot of stuff?" Jan asked, wondering if this guy was as weird as he sounded.

"Not so far." Liam adjusted his sunglasses, which had slid down his head. "You said your 'new' step-dad. Your folks haven't been married long?"

She debated how much to tell her nosy partner, and then decided it wouldn't hurt to fill him in. The details of her life weren't exactly earth-shaking news. "My mom and David McKenna, who was a Bragg Creek police constable then, began dating after my big brother Grey was in a nasty motorcycle accident last year. David went with us to the hospital, helped out, and stepped up when he had to." She thought of the trouble her brother had been in with the law back then, and was once again glad David had been there. "They announced they were getting married, David joined the RCMP, and that's how the Fournier-McKenna family landed here. End of story."

"So you and your brother Grey are both into motorcycles? I mean, I happened to notice you ride to school … on a great-looking bike."

He seemed embarrassed and Jan realized he'd just admitted to doing more than noticing her around once or twice.

"Does your brother live with you?" Liam went on too quickly as though trying to cover his faux pas.

"No, Grey lives in Bragg Creek. He's great."

Jan's face clouded over. She missed her brother a lot. "He owns a new motorcycle repair and prep shop. Grey's a magician with bikes. In fact, he's building a killer-fast race bike for me to ride in the big Western Canada Road Race Championship near the end of May. He's going to invite some factory reps and sports writers to watch. If I kick butt, we'll have all the publicity for his shop and sponsorship for racing we'll ever need. It's huge."

Liam rubbed the back of his neck. "Do you mind me asking where you come from originally? I mean, your skin and hair ..."

His voice trailed off and Jan felt the old shields go up. She was Metis, a blend of First Nations and European ancestry, but in her case, the deep end of the gene pool was her First Nations side. She hated having to explain the colour of her skin like she had some kind of control over how she'd ended up looking. She turned to Liam, a caustic remark on the tip of her tongue, then saw there was no malice in his eyes. She blew out the breath she'd been unconsciously holding. "My people came from right here. I'm Metis, a made-in-Canada original."

A look of comprehension came over Liam's face and he grinned. "Metis! Right — your burnished copper skin, that glossy black hair," he teased. "And those wicked dark-chocolate eyes. How could I have missed it?"

Jan blushed under his onslaught of dopey compliments. "That's me: part red, part white, like

Canada's flag. I take after *nohkôm*, my grandmother," she explained. "She's Cree." She decided to shift the conversation. "How about you? Are you from Banff?"

Liam's attitude immediately cooled and he shook his head mutely. Reaching out, he stabbed the power button on the monitor to turn it off. "No, my mom and I moved here after my parents divorced five years ago. I don't see my dad much. He sends me tons of gifts, though." He pulled the sunglasses down in front of his face. "Like these million-dollar shades that are supposed to make up for cancelling on me this summer. We were going to hike the West Coast Trail on Vancouver Island, but something more important came up." Jan heard the sting of bitterness. "Where'd your dad end up after your parents divorced?"

Jan felt the colour drain from her face. "My dad?" She was momentarily flustered. "He … he died." This was a subject she never talked about. She glanced at her watch, her irritation at this computer nerd flooded back in a big way. "I've got to get home for supper. We have an RCMP summer student coming to live with us and I'm part of the welcoming committee." She jumped up so quickly, her chair nearly tipped over.

"A what?" Liam called, but Jan was already hurrying out of the classroom.

Chapter 2

"Honey, she's here!"

Jan heard her mother calling and shut off her computer. It was just as well. She'd been trying to think of a great topic for the web site, one even B. Liam Simpson couldn't shoot down, but wasn't having any luck.

Racing downstairs, Jan slammed out the back door in time to see their new boarder pull into the driveway … on a big, boomy motorcycle! She studied the sleek lines of the Kawasaki ZX-10R, a lightning-fast bike that would leave the others reading your back plate. Awesome! Getting to know their boarder could have some great perks, like talking bikes to someone who rode a rocket.

Jan stood beside her tall, dark-haired stepfather. Ever since they'd arrived in Banff, David had been working more and more hours, and Jan worried he worked too much. He had come straight from work and was still in his RCMP uniform, but he was here to greet the summer student.

The leather-jacketed rider shut off her bike and flipped up the visor on her pearl-white helmet. It glinted in the light. "Hi, I'm Willow Whitecloud," the young woman announced. "Is it okay if I park my bike here in the driveway? I'd rather not leave it on the street."

Jan immediately liked Willow. She obviously had her priorities straight. Willow was looking at the tires on her motorcycle, stained with red mud that left a rusty mess on the concrete. Jan thought of all the good old Alberta topsoil she'd tracked in over the years and knew her mom wouldn't mind.

"Of course." Jan's mom smiled. "I'm used to a little motorcycle mess. What's a little more? I'm Violet Fournier." The petite black-haired woman held out her hand as Willow hastily pulled off her helmet and glove before shaking it.

Willow unstrapped her duffle bag from the back of her bike, then followed Jan's mom up the driveway to where the rest of the family waited. "This is my husband, David McKenna, and this is my daughter January."

"Glad you made it here safely." David greeted Willow warmly. "It's a long ride from Edmonton."

"Cool bike. Have you had it long?" Jan enthused, admiring the shiny blue bullet. "Does it really top out at 186 mph, like the mags say?"

Willow's eyes shone. "I know it's not as practical as a car, but it's way more fun. And yes, this bike will make you a believer. Do you ride?"

"That's my R6," Jan jerked her thumb in the direction of the open garage.

"Sweet!" Willow's gaze took in Jan's ride.

Violet Fournier sighed. "Another motorcycle nut, exactly what this house needs! Now, let's have supper. You girls can talk shop later."

After one last appreciative look at Willow's ZX, Jan followed the others inside.

* * *

"So what's this RCMP summer student program about, Willow?" Jan reached for more of her mom's delicious venison roast. "Do you get to do actual police work like my stepdad?"

Willow also took another slice. "The program rocks! It lets the students experience policing first-hand." She added a scoop of mashed potatoes to her plate. "Being chosen this year wasn't easy. Out of all the applicants, only seven were selected for the national program. Since I was number eight on the magic list, I opted for K Division and am one of the thirty-five students in that."

David offered her a bowl of vegetables. "If I remember rightly, there was something else different about the two programs?"

Willow smiled wryly. "Only one important detail. In the national program, the feds pick up the tab; in K Division, you have to come up with your own funds. I borrowed from everyone I know to make it here. And I came into a little cash, which helped." Using her fork like a scalpel, she carefully shaped her mashed potatoes into a dollar sign. "The training itself was intense. We had basics in the use of force and self-defence, law, community policing, drug awareness, and radio procedures. It totally prepares you for the street."

David set the bowl down. "I enjoyed my training and it sounds like you did too."

A thoughtful look crossed Willow's face. "It was tough, but you know something? I did enjoy it."

"The whole thing sounds like a blast," Jan agreed. "Do you get to wear an official uniform?"

"We wear modified RCMP uniforms — the biggest modification being that we don't have guns!" Willow laughed.

Jan was intrigued. "What about taking down bad guys? Did they teach you stuff like that?"

Willow nodded. "Oh, for sure. This is the big league."

"Your reserve is at Rainbow Lake?" Violet Fournier asked, nudging the conversation in another direction.

"North of Rainbow, actually. Deep in the bush or, as we say, the Land of Muskeg, where the black fly is king." Willow wiped her mouth with her napkin before folding it neatly. "That was delicious, Mrs. Fournier. I live," she corrected herself, "I mean, I *lived* with *Nimosôm*, my grandfather, before he passed away. Cooking wasn't one of the gifts the Great Spirit gave him. I haven't had a meal this good since, well, ever. *Kinanâskomitin*, thank you."

Jan's mom beamed. "It's nice to hear Cree again. Please, call me Violet."

"Oh, David, I nearly forgot!" Jan interrupted as she looked at her stepdad. "Please, please, please remember my big school thing coming up. It's called *Extreme Careers — Do You Dare?* And you're my first star speaker. I kind of want you to be huge. After this series, I'm sure to get a great mark in my life skills course."

David smiled reassuringly. "It's your brain-child, Jan. You should get an A, or even an A-plus."

Jan's mom pushed her chair back from the table. "Honey, why don't you show Willow her room and help her unpack while David and I clean up."

They were giving Willow the room next to Jan's in the converted attic space, the room that would have been Grey's if he were still living with them. Jan missed her brother a lot, but knew how important his new motorcycle shop was to him. He was happy in Bragg Creek, and if Jan did well in the May race, she was sure his fledgling business would be a success.

"I hope you didn't go to too much trouble, Mrs. Fournier. I mean, Violet." Willow said politely. "Accommodation is hard to find in Banff, so when the detachment said you'd offered me a place to stay, I couldn't refuse. I'm very grateful to be staying in your wonderful home."

Right on, thought Jan. Her mom liked that super-polite stuff. Making herself and Willow scarce sounded good to Jan. "Come on, Willow. I'll help you stow your gear."

Willow turned dark eyes to David. "I was hoping to ask you about the spring grizzly bear hunt, Constable McKenna. I'm interested in how it's going."

He stood up. "It's *David*. And sure, since you're one of us," he smiled at the reference to Willow's special RCMP status, "I'd be happy to fill you in. But right now I have to get back before they send out the cavalry." He shrugged apologetically to his wife. "Sorry, Vi, but I can't help you with kitchen duty."

Just then, there was a sharp rap on the back door. David opened it and looked surprised to see Corporal Dirk Sloan, his superior officer. "I know I said I was taking a long supper break, Grizz, but you didn't have to come and get me," David joked. Jan thought the nickname suited the burly officer. His hat seemed to float atop his coarse brown hair, and his bushy moustache added to the overall bearish effect.

"David, we've had a bear poaching," Sloan explained. "The park warden's office called and reported a fresh grizzly kill. They used a high-powered rifle, then harvested the body parts. The warden said the carcass was a real mess."

David was immediately all business. Sloan continued. "Since you're the liaison between the RCMP and the warden's office, I need you to check it out. I'm going to talk to Todd Dyer, the guide who works at Wapiti Trail Outfitters. He had an expensive hunting rifle stolen a couple of days ago and, if we can match the ballistics, we'll at least know if that's the gun being used."

"Have you any idea who the poacher is?" Willow interrupted.

David picked his peaked cap up off the counter. "Grizz, this is our new summer student Willow Whitecloud. She starts tomorrow. Willow, this is Corporal Sloan."

"Welcome to Banff detachment, Whitecloud. You're assigned to work with me, so I guess I'll see you bright and early in the morning." Sloan rested his hand on the holster of his sidearm. "As far as the poaching goes, we're just starting the investigation. Maybe Constable McKenna here will get lucky and find some clue as to who's responsible." Sloan turned to Jan's mom and touched the brim of his hat. "Sorry to interrupt your dinner, Violet."

Jan's mom looked resigned. "Don't worry about it, Dirk. All part of my husband's new career." She smiled at David. "I won't wait up."

Willow went to the window and watched as the two officers left.

Jan felt sick. The idea of some maniac killing bears in Banff was horrible. The bears were the heart and soul of the park, and everyone took a serious interest in their welfare. With a sudden flash, she knew what their computer project should be. It was a gigabyte idea, and she could hardly wait to see that arrogant B. Liam Simpson, king of the computer geeks, again. Even he would be on board. Jan felt bubbly with anticipation as she and Willow cleared the table.

* * *

"It's too bad David had to leave, but poaching is a nasty business." Willow followed Jan up the narrow stairs tucked in the corner of the kitchen that led to their tiny attic rooms.

"It sucks, especially in the park where animals are protected." Jan walked down the short hallway to the farthest door. "Home sweet home. It's cramped, but cozy. The rest of the house is also small, but really comfortable. My favourite thing is the wood-burning fireplaces in each bedroom and the living room." She motioned to the steeply sloped ceilings. "It's typical Banff style, so the roof will shed the snow. You'll get used to it after you bump your head a couple of times."

As Jan stowed Willow's new RCMP uniform in the closet, she hoped the wrinkles would fall out before she wore the tunic the next day. She knew how picky David was about his uniform.

She flopped down on the bed and watched as Willow finished her unpacking. "You said you used to live with your grandfather. Are your parents dead?" The question was out before Jan had a chance to wonder if she was being rude. It did not seem to faze Willow.

"Actually, my parents are both alive, as far as I know. They left to get a six-pack when I was a baby and haven't come back yet."

Jan was taken aback at the brutal honesty of this answer. "David is my stepfather. My real dad died when I was little," she blurted, embarrassed at making Willow reveal something so personal, and wanting things to ease up a bit. But then she couldn't stop herself asking an even more personal question. "Do you ever wonder if they'll come back?"

"No. My parents won't be coming back. I accepted this a long time ago," Willow answered without anger or resentment in her voice. "For years I said I knew they were gone for good, but in my heart I secretly hoped they'd come back for me. Letting go is hard, but once you do it, your life's journey can go forward."

"Sometimes I pretend my dad's gone on a trip and I'm waiting for him." Jan picked up a curious-looking deerskin bag from the bed. "Where do you want this?"

"That's my medicine bundle. I'll take it." Willow reached for the pouch, but when her hand touched Jan's, she stopped. The look on her face was knowing, as though she and Jan suddenly shared a secret. "With your Metis roots, I think you'll be interested in what I have in here."

Willow felt in the bag and withdrew a handful of squares of coloured cloth. "The red goes to the south for Mr. Mouse." She placed the cloth on one side of the wide dresser and set a small figure of a mouse on it. "The white to the north, with the buffalo of course." She placed this cloth opposite the red square and put a handful of brown fluff on it. Jan figured it was bison hair. "The yellow in the east with the eagle." Willow put a brown feather on this square. "In the centre, Mother Earth." She put a green swatch in the middle and placed a clay bowl on it. "And the west belongs to the mighty bear. He has the blue square." She reverently put the blue cloth down, then went to her leather motorcycle jacket and rummaged in the pocket. Jan watched as Willow withdrew a pouch of tobacco, opened it, and sprinkled the contents on the five cloths. Next she pulled a braid of sweetgrass and a bunch of sage out of the bag. The room was immediately filled with the pungent fragrance of the sacred herbs.

Jan knew that these items were important. She didn't understand much about the religious teachings, but did know First Nations spiritual beliefs were tied closely to the Earth and all things on it.

Willow whispered several words in Cree, then placed the sweetgrass in Jan's hand. "Mother Earth's hair."

Jan smiled; her mother called the dried grass bundles the same thing. She brought the fragrant braid to her nose, closed her eyes, and inhaled.

Instantly, in her mind, she was standing in a sunny field surrounded by prairie grass. She could feel the summer sun on her face and the warm earth beneath her feet. Her eyes flew open in surprise. She could have sworn the soles of her feet actually felt hot!

Jan stared at the sweetgrass, remembering the hospital room after Grey's accident. David had brought a woven braid of sweetgrass to help her gravely injured brother heal.

Jan had been raised Roman Catholic, and since the accident she had gone to mass regularly. Pleased, her mom had given Jan the family rosary of worn stone beads that had belonged to January's grandmother. It made Jan feel that she was part of a tradition that went back a long way. When she'd first gone to church, she found it extremely comforting to sit in the old wooden pew, surrounded by the stillness and statues, and let the feeling of peace and sanctuary enfold her. It had helped Jan with the bad memories that sometimes crept into her dreams.

But these days, that warm feeling took a while to kick in. Instead, she felt uneasy, like she'd missed something important. She thought of the shadowy figure that haunted her dreams and felt a chill run down her spine. The phantom would move toward something unknown that terrified Jan. When she tried to clutch the figure, to save it, her fingers closed on icy emptiness. Whatever waited in the darkness, she was powerless to stop it. She would wake with a desperate feeling that she had let something terrible happen.

"It does the same thing to me."

The sound of Willow's voice jolted Jan back from her dark thoughts. She turned to look questioningly at the young woman.

Willow nodded at the sweetgrass. "It conjures up memories, always reminds me of summer."

"What? Oh, yes." Jan exhaled loudly as she gently placed the braid on the dresser. "Strange, isn't it, how smells can make you remember things." She looked at Willow. "Is this," she indicated the various articles, "part of your religion, what you believe in?"

Willow's eyes had an inner fire when she answered. "These are powerful things, January. Nimosôm was a shaman and a medicine man; he healed people inside and out." Her fingers lovingly caressed each object as she arranged them on the dresser. "He taught me the old ways, that all life is sacred and nature holds secrets we don't understand."

"Does this stuff work?" Jan looked at the array skeptically.

Willow hesitated. "It's complicated, not a matter of simply handing out a bottle of pills. But, bottom line, yes." She went to her medicine bundle and pulled out one last item. It was wrapped in brown hide with hair on it.

"Is that bearskin?" Jan watched Willow carefully unwrap the object.

"Yes, grizzly hide. And this," Willow withdrew a small lifelike statue of a bear and placed it on the square of blue cloth on the dresser, "is very valuable. Some of my people have spent their lives as guardians of the bears."

Jan glanced at Willow's face and for an instant, it was as though a cloud had passed in front of the sun. Willow's eyes grew cold and hard, then she blinked and everything was the same again.

Jan stared. Encircling the bear was a necklace of what had to be a hundred grizzly claws, each matched in colour and size as perfectly as pearls in a necklace. The curved claws were extremely long and looked razor-sharp. January had never seen anything like it.

Chapter 3

Despite it being Saturday and a perfect opportunity to sleep in, Jan was up early the next morning. There was no sound from the new boarder's room and she wondered if Willow had overslept. Being late was no way to start your first day on the job. She was about to knock on Willow's door when it opened.

"Good morning, Willow," Jan said cheerily. "I thought maybe you'd slept through your alarm, but I can see you've been up for a while." She noticed most of the wrinkles had fallen out of Willow's uniform. "You look spit-and-polish ready." Glancing past Willow, Jan saw a laptop computer sitting on the desk, with a phone line running to a jack in the wall. Dial-up was slow but would let Willow access the Internet and check her e-mail messages from back home.

"I feel like somebody's *ohkomimâw* grandmother, with this do, but my hair has to be off the collar." Willow turned to show Jan a tightly rolled bun at the nape of her neck. "Is it too gross?" She patted her hair, fingering a newly escaped tendril dangling behind her ear.

"Don't worry. You look great, cutting edge. Ready for breakfast?" Jan started to turn.

"Two seconds while I fix this stupid hair." Fuming, Willow went back into her room and stood in front of the mirror to refasten the wild strand. "It's a good thing I don't have to go through a metal detector. With all these pins stuck in my head, I'd have the whole place locked down in no time."

Jan noticed Willow had left her laptop running and walked over to the desk. She was about to offer to turn it off when the image on the screen drew her eye. It was a map of Banff National Park with lots of coloured dots on it. "What's the map with the polka dots for?"

Willow hurried to her computer and started to shut it down. "Oh, hey, I forgot I'd left it on. Thanks for reminding me."

"The map and the dots …" Jan looked at the screen more closely before it went dark.

"Oh, those. They're tourist sights I plan to see while I'm here. I don't want to miss anything before I go back north. If you've got the time, maybe you could be my tour guide." Willow snapped the computer shut. "Come on. I'm starved."

Jan sniffed. The room had a pungent smell she hadn't noticed before. "Have you been burning something?"

"Only my smudge stick," Willow said casually. "I burn it when I say my morning and evening blessing. I couldn't sleep here last night until I purified the room, especially the corners. My grandfather worried that there was a *wittigo* looking for me. He made me promise to be extra diligent with my prayers."

"A *wittigo*? What's that?" Jan's curiosity was piqued.

"A *wittigo* is an evil spirit that is made of wood, or ice, or maybe mud. It eats human flesh. Darn hard to kill." Willow started for the stairs. "Coming?"

Speechless, Jan followed. Evil spirits, magic coloured cloth, burning grass … It seemed they had a witch doctor for a boarder!

David was in the kitchen when the girls entered. He'd returned late at night, and Jan thought he looked extremely tired. Pulling four mugs out of the cupboard, she poured the coffee as her mother bustled into the kitchen.

"I'll take that coffee in a go-cup, Honey. I have an early meeting." Her mom kissed her on the cheek then gave David an even quicker kiss. "See you two," she smiled at Willow, "Sorry, *three,* later."

Jan's mother worked for a large insurance company. She was kept busy, but loved the challenging schedule.

"David, did you find out anything about the poacher?" Willow asked, pouring a generous amount of vanilla-flavoured creamer into her coffee.

"Maybe," David said. "We're not finished sifting through the clues."

"Does the calibre of the bullets match the stolen gun?" Willow asked.

David rubbed his eyes tiredly. "We're waiting for a ballistics report, but the chances of the stolen rifle being the one that was used should be easy to prove. The rifle was an odd calibre, a special German make."

"Is the ballistics lab in Calgary?" Willow asked.

"Yes, but they're fast on turnaround. We should have something concrete soon." David finished his coffee. "Usually park wardens handle animal calls. We get involved if there are violations, such as a poacher using a firearm illegally or selling bear parts. Then we work as a team to apprehend the bad guys." He set his mug down. "And speaking of bad guys, I'd better get to work. Willow, can I give you a ride in?"

Willow hesitated. "Actually, I think I'll take my bike. I have a couple of errands to run before my big first day."

Willow grabbed her motorcycle gear out of the closet and was about to follow David when Jan stopped her. "I'm going to see my brother in Bragg Creek later. If you're off, you could come. I know some back roads, and it would be a blast, especially with that wicked ride of yours."

"Sounds like a great way to relax," Willow agreed. "I'll meet you here at four." She yanked her leather jacket on over her uniform and left.

Not wanting her mom or David to come home

to a mess, Jan washed the breakfast dishes and scrubbed the counter until it shone. She opened the refrigerator door to put the milk away, then took a quick swig from the carton. No sense in making another glass dirty and, besides, her mom wasn't there to lecture her on proper etiquette.

She tipped the carton too far and milk spilled out of the edges, running down her chin. "Rats!" She shook the dribbles off her T-shirt, then, using her stockinged foot, swiped at the milk freckles scattered across the floor. Noticing Willow had left her backpack near the door, Jan thought she'd do the new boarder a favour and put it in her room. When she picked up the pack, a thin strip of paper fell to the floor.

It was a Banff National Park pass, dated two days before. Jan wondered why, if Willow had arrived then, she hadn't come to their house until yesterday. Maybe she had to make sure the coast was clear and there were no *wittigos* or Winnebagos lurking around. Jan tucked the pass back into the bag.

* * *

Ten minutes later, Jan climbed on her bike and headed to Liam's house to work on their web site. She didn't really feel comfortable going to his place, but Liam said he preferred to work on his own computer. The only other choice was to wait until school on Monday, and Jan couldn't wait that long; not when she had the world's best topic for their project.

As she wended her way down the crowded streets, Jan had to admit that Banff was aces, with camping and hiking in the summer and the best skiing and snowboarding in the winter. Set in the heart of Alberta's Rocky Mountains, it was filled with picturesque stone buildings and colourful hanging flower baskets that kept tourists' cameras clicking. On any day Jan could hear a dozen different languages being spoken as she strolled down the street.

She stopped for a red light and grinned. The traffic lights on Banff's main street were the best. They had a pixel countdown of the seconds left before they changed. A girl knew exactly when to pop the clutch.

As Jan waited for the light, her eye was caught by a familiar figure standing in Wapiti Trail Outfitters on the corner. It was Willow.

Jan flipped up the visor on her helmet and squinted. This must have been one of the errands Willow mentioned. She watched as Mr. Dyer handed Willow a brown paper bag, then spent a long time completing the transaction on the till. Seeing their new boarder shopping let Jan see her more like a normal teenage girl, instead of an apprentice RCMP officer.

A horn honked, cueing Jan that the light had changed. She snapped her visor closed and shifted into gear.

When she arrived at Liam's house, he greeted her at the front door with a tray of sodas and cookies. "This way to the Wizard's Lair." He opened the door wide and Jan walked into a tidy living room, then followed Liam upstairs. She suspected they were going to his room and a brief flash of panic hit her.

The sight of a black door with a skull and crossbones painted in red did nothing to lessen her nervousness. "Uh, maybe we should work downstairs."

"Can't." Liam opened the door. "My computer is in here."

Jan leaned hesitantly forward and peeked into the room. She expected a totally trashed, clothes everywhere, posters-plastered-on-the-wall kind of place, and was surprised when she saw that Liam's room was tidier than her own — even, she decided with chagrin, better decorated.

"I may be a geek," he glanced at Jan like he knew that's what she called him, and she flushed guiltily. "But since all I care about is my computer, it doesn't kill me to keep the rest of the room the way my mom likes it." Liam motioned to a small alcove to the left of the door.

Jan couldn't suppress a smile. This was more like it. The walls were painted black to match the door, and there was a large poster of Einstein pinned to the ceiling. Computer disks and stacks of manuals were everywhere, as well as racks holding hundreds of computer program disks and home-burned CDs. A steering wheel attached to the computer by cables was stuffed under the desk next to a set of pedals, and Jan guessed they were to simulate the brake and accelerator on a car.

"Better," she said out loud. This was more what she would have expected from a seventeen-year-old guy. Then she spotted, stuck to the side of the hard drive, a Japanese cartoon image of a scantily clad girl with an abundant chest. "She looks … healthy."

Embarrassed, Liam bustled forward with his tray and set it down on a pile of magazines. Jan glimpsed the top title — *Cyber-Trash* — before it was covered by their snack. "I may not be perfect but, to quote Data, 'I fall within normal operating parameters.' That Anime," he tipped his head toward the buxom action figure. "She's the lead character in a game I play with a couple of buddies on the Internet."

Jan hesitated, then grabbed a stack of computer game disks off a chair, moved them to a tiny side table, and sat down. "Hey, I don't care how you waste your time. But right now I want to work on our project, so let's get started." Her prudish tone made her wince. That wasn't her at all.

"Right!" He bumped the mouse, bringing the screen to life, then keyed in the sequence to open their untitled, no-topic web page.

Jan tried to contain her excitement. "I have the best idea for our site. Wait till you hear this …" She paused, expecting some kind of response, but Liam only continued looking at the computer screen. "Liam!" Jan said loudly.

"What? Oh, right. Big idea. Can't wait. Yadda, yadda … Okay, what is it?" He looked at her, fingers poised over his keyboard as though she'd interrupted him in the middle of an earth-shattering, universe-ending critical sentence.

Jan took a deep breath. "I want to do a project on tracking the park bears. You know, the ones that have the special radio collars tracked by the Government of Alberta Fish and Wildlife. Kids from all over the world could see how our bears really live."

Liam looked at her. "Bears?" He thought about it for a minute and Jan thought he was going to give her grief. Then he nodded. "Right on. They're all numbered so we could have a page for each bruin. I like it. January, you're a genius."

He smiled at her, a warm and genuine smile that made Jan feel a small unexpected shiver of pleasure. The reaction flustered her. Guys and she did not mix, especially when the guy was an egomaniac computer geek!

Liam's fingers started typing. "Brilliant! We'll document where the bears wander, where they sleep, what they eat. And when they interact with humans, what the outcome was."

"We could have maps and show how their habitat is disappearing. Pictures of roly-poly bear cubs will win us points with the girls for sure." Jan was excited now.

As Liam typed at a furious pace, Jan got her first look at the screen. She raised her eyebrows.

"We can't call our web site *that*!" The folder was labelled "The Jan and Liam Gong Show." "We need something more woodsy-bearsy-Banffsy." She reached for one of the shortbread cookies on the tray. "Hey, how about 'Paws in the Park, Bare Facts about Factual Bears?'" She took a big bite of the cookie.

"Sounds corny enough even Mr. Volk will love it." Liam's fingers flashed and their web site was born. He added a note for early visitors: "Under Construction, Please Bear With Us!"

"The Alberta Fish and Wildlife web site should have megabytes of info we can download." Liam looked thoughtful. "A worthy challenge."

Jan wondered what this meant. "I can interview local guides and outfitters for more data." She was feeling good about this project. Liam was being a huge asset.

As they reviewed their progress, Jan sipped her soda and had several more of the great-tasting cookies. Another way she differed from her classmates was that she wasn't constantly watching every calorie. The snack hit the spot and she started to relax, despite the fact that she was in Liam's bedroom.

"You said something about getting a new RCMP boarder. How'd that turn out?" Liam finished typing in the string of keystrokes, the HTML code for their web-site program.

"She's an RCMP summer student in this program I'd never heard of before." Briefly, Jan told him about Willow, the RCMP program, and the strange items they'd unpacked. "And she believes in evil spirits and smudges herself morning and night! A real weird case, just this side of crazy."

"So?" Liam shrugged. "Everybody believes in something. I'm always saying a prayer to the Great Sysadmin in the sky to save me from the blue screen of death, nasty viruses, or some bit-head hacking my PC." He tucked his sunglasses up on his head. "I've seen you at St. Mary's on Sundays, so I'm guessing a religious belief isn't new to you."

Jan was taken aback. "You've seen me at mass?" She started to wonder if Liam was some kind of stalker. And here she was, sitting in his bedroom!

"My brother is the parish priest here. That's one of the reasons my mom decided to move to Banff. We all need a support system and, after dad cut out and left us high and dry, Jeremy was it for the Simpson clan."

Jan heard that bitterness again and decided that talking about Liam's family life was probably not a good thing to do. She switched topics. "Willow does have a wicked bike, though. Man, I bet that thing howls!"

"Yeah, yeah, concentrate on the important stuff." He changed a couple of the symbols on the screen. "Our primo web site. How'd you come up with this whole track-the-bears idea anyway?" He turned to stare at her.

His eyes sparkled like blue glacier ice. "Ah, actually, it was because of what happened yesterday." Jan felt her stomach tighten. "There was a poaching here in the park. Someone shot a grizzly and harvested it."

Liam stared at her in shock. "You're kidding! Some creep killed a bear for parts? That's so slimy. Unbelievable. Guns are totally illegal in a national park. They even have to be disassembled for travel. Have they got whoever did it?"

"Hey, I'm not CNN! I told you what I know, which is not much. When I heard about it, I knew the bears needed us to tell their story."

The computer screen flashed and a pop-up ad suddenly appeared.

"Man, I thought my new firewall would take care of these." Liam hit a couple of keys and the ad disappeared. "More homework for me."

"I get those all the time. They have to be the most annoying things on the Internet. And my computer crashes every time they show up." Jan shook her head. "Unfortunately, I don't have your talent for getting rid of the pests."

"The point is, I shouldn't be getting them at all." His fingers whizzed over the keyboard. "I knew it!" He leaned forward, his eyes intent on the message scrolling across the screen. "A hacker buddy of mine thought it would be a huge joke to punch a hole in my security, then send me a couple of ads just to tick me off. This means war!" He began typing at a furious rate.

Jan checked her watch and couldn't believe she'd been at Liam's for hours. She still had some things to do before she met Willow for their ride to Bragg Creek. "I have to go now." She stood up to leave.

"Ah, okay. Give me a minute." Liam's eyes never left the screen.

"Don't get up. I can find my way out." Liam now seemed oblivious to the fact that Jan was in the same universe, let alone leaving his room. The way he moved in cyberspace and his reference to a hacker buddy made her wonder about what darker uses he put his talents to. She remembered his comment about the Fish and Wildlife site. What worthy challenge? She closed the front door behind her.

Buckling up her helmet, Jan started her bike. As she rode home, Liam's words about everyone believing in something came back to her. It wasn't that she didn't believe, it was simply that she wasn't sure what it was she believed in. In school, they'd studied different religions from around the world, but none of them really touched her. Jan thought of Willow and her belief in the old ways. Now, that was different.

Chapter 4

It was a perfect afternoon for a ride, and, as Jan opened up the throttle, she felt her bike's 600cc engine respond. The agile R6 sport bike was nimble and reacted faster than her old modified '86 RZ350. Jan sped forward, expertly weaving through the slower traffic as she and Willow blasted down the wide Trans-Canada Highway. Jan glimpsed Willow in her mirrors. Willow's ZX was far more powerful than Jan's bike, but Jan knew Willow wasn't pushing it anywhere near its top end.

The smooth vibration from her bike's engine made Jan's bones hum with a resonance like a bow being drawn across a violin string. Every muscle was in perfect harmony with the fast bike. Suddenly, with a wave of her gloved hand, Willow flashed by. The Kawasaki's monster motor howled, and the blue bullet disappeared like it had warp drive. "That's more like it!" Jan yelled.

Jan watched Willow's tail light disappearing. She'd never catch the ZX in a straight line, but there was a stretch of road before Bragg Creek that was curvy and had corners her bike would slide through like silk. Jan flattened herself over the tank, cutting the wind resistance. She'd get Willow there.

Jan concentrated on squeezing every one of the 108 horses out of her engine. Ahead, Willow was still pulling away. Far in the distance, Jan could see the tightly twisting section she'd been waiting for. As she'd predicted, Willow's brake light winked on well before the first corner and Jan knew she'd be gearing down.

Jan glanced at her digital speedometer and saw she was pushing the 230 kph mark. Waiting until the last possible moment, she squeezed her brake lever, then blasted into the turn. Clipping the apex, she quickly ate up the ground between her and Willow, who'd entered the set of corners like she was under a full course caution. Jan reeled the ZX in.

Willow never saw her coming. Leaning hard over, Jan's slider grazed the hot pavement as she deftly danced through the corners, slowed to the posted speed, then waited for Willow to catch up. When the girls parked their bikes in front of Grey's shop, they were both laughing from the exhilarating ride.

"That was a blast!" Jan said breathlessly. "I think I pushed my R6 harder than I ever have." Her lips twitched up at the corners. "On the street, that is."

"About time!" Grey's deep voice made Jan spin around.

"Hey, big brother," Jan smiled broadly. "Meet Willow Whitecloud. Willow, this is my brother, Grey Fournier. Grey, Willow and I raced up here. It was fantastic!"

"Hi, Willow. Jan's trying to make me jealous. My racing days are over." He held his arm up. "Permanently wrecked wrist. I leave the racing to my kid sister, who can pilot our silver bullet faster than any bike jockey out there."

"Jan's a wicked rider." Willow rubbed the back of her left leg. "The ZX rocks, but it has the nasty habit of heating up this leg on a long ride. I guess it's true, there are no perfect bikes."

Grey admired her gleaming machine. "Super set of wheels."

Jan punched her brother on the shoulder. "How about showing Willow our secret weapon?"

He led them to the back of the spotless garage where a brand new YZF R6 waited. The silver bike with black flames running down the tank looked white-hot, even sitting still.

Willow whistled. "Wow! You're going to race that crotch rocket, Jan?"

"Yup. If my brother can figure out how to tweak the new Ohlin suspension kit he put on and fine tune the exhaust system he's been raving about." She gave Grey an inquiring look.

"The new breathing system should give it more power. That and Jan's great riding skills will make us a sure winner at the competition in May. A win would put Eaglefeather Racing on the map." Grey looked at his sister. "*If* you get in the practice time I scheduled."

"I'm trying, but school is tough, and Mom will freak if my grades slip because I'm on the track."

"Okay. I don't want your marks to go in the dumpster either. Can you ditch any extracurricular activities, like a boyfriend?" Grey tossed the rag he'd been using to wipe his hands onto the workbench.

For some reason, Jan thought of Liam. "I don't have any dumb boyfriend," she protested. "Or any other diversions. It's school and the race, period. And speaking of the race, let's get that baby of yours revved." She yanked her helmet back on and started over to the waiting race bike.

The section of disused road that was their makeshift track was a short drive from Bragg Creek. Willow and Grey followed Jan in the beat-up old pickup that was Grey's main form of transportation now. Jan and the bike performed beautifully as she pushed herself and her machine harder than ever before. The race-prepped bike was incredibly responsive. It seemed all she had to do was think what she wanted it to do, and it leaped to obey. Satisfied, Jan took the bike back to the shop and parked it.

"Wow!" Willow said as Jan pulled her helmet off. "The Creator has given you a real talent."

"Willow believes in the old ways," Jan

explained to Grey. "So don't tick her off or she'll send a wicked, wailing *wittigo* after you." The look of shock on Willow's face made Jan realize she shouldn't have said that.

Willow looked directly into Jan's eyes. When she spoke there was a power, almost a force, in her voice. "I wouldn't joke about these things. They're always listening … and waiting."

"Sorry, Willow," Jan apologized, a little flustered. "I didn't mean anything." She wondered how strongly the young Cree woman believed in what Jan had seen in her room.

When the subject of supper came up, Jan naturally picked Robin's Mountain Bistro, where she used to work. While they sat down and ordered, Jan and Willow talked about Native religious beliefs. Native beliefs with their respect for nature seemed to make perfect sense to Jan. Grey leaned back and listened quietly as the girls continued their discussion and drank the coffee they'd ordered, but sat up when their pizza arrived.

"How's life treating my best ex-server?" Robin asked Jan, setting the large Bragg Special pizza they'd ordered onto the table.

"Okay." Jan didn't want to go into how she was worried about David working so much, or that she was teamed with B. Liam Simpson, computer guru and suspected hacker, in order to bag a good grade! Instead, she deflected the attention to the new boarder. "Robin, this is Willow Whitecloud from Rainbow Lake. She's staying with us until the fall. Willow's in the RCMP's summer student program, kind of like an apprentice cop."

"Hi, Willow. That sounds like a more interesting summer job than bussing tables," Robin laughed. "Are you doing anything exciting at this new job?"

Willow shook her head. "I'm working with this real tough guy, Corporal Sloan. He's a stickler for procedure. I also volunteered to do some computer data entry for Alberta Fish and Wildlife on the spring grizzly bear hunt, cross-checking names with WINs, Wildlife Identification Numbers, drawn for the hunt."

"The spring hunt is very controversial around here," Robin said with a frown.

Willow nodded. "Yeah, some people think hunting prevents overpopulation, but others think it's a waste of a vanishing species."

"Which camp are you in?" Jan asked.

Instead of answering, Willow tipped her empty coffee cup and looked into the bottom. "My grandfather said often the side you choose depends on the amount of money at stake."

Robin turned to Jan's brother. "Speaking of the hunt … Grey, was your number picked in the spring grizzly draw?"

Grey sighed theatrically. "Nah, but that means my WIN moves up a notch for next year. Eventually, I'll get my turn."

The restaurant owner's feathery brows knit in the middle again. "It's the darndest thing, but I don't know one hunter from around here who was successful this year. It's odd. But who knows, maybe all the lucky ones came from up around your area, Willow."

Willow set the last of her pizza slice back on her plate. "I don't think there's a lot of luck anywhere this year."

Chapter 5

As everyone became accustomed to one another, life settled into a new routine at Jan's house. A lot of the time, the house was empty. There'd been two more bears killed and the hunt for the poachers was now the topic of conversation at every coffee kiosk in Banff. Jan was kept busy with her school project and practising for the race. The clock was ticking and race day was less than a month away.

Willow came and went at irregular hours. When Jan would hear her come in late at night, Willow would tell her she'd been sampling the nightlife. Willow was amazed at how many clubs there were for a town this size, but Jan just laughed and told her it was just an average tourist mecca.

Jan was also building up a tolerance to B. Liam Simpson. Working with him was a lot like wearing a new wool sweater. It looked good, but it itched. However, Jan told herself she could get used to anything, even someone who rubbed her the wrong way, especially if that someone was a computer genius who was going to help her get a super grade.

* * *

Jan slept late Sunday morning and had to scramble to get ready for church. David had missed the week before because of the poaching case, and her mom insisted they all had to go to mass together this time. Jan had noticed she had started to feel different about attending church. Going was okay and so was leaving; it was the in-between part that was hard. She couldn't seem to focus on what Father Simpson was saying.

"Hey, Willow, you want to come to mass with us this morning?" Jan called from the open doorway of her room as she tried to brush her hair into submission.

Willow sat on the floor in the middle of her room, the smudge bowl in front of her. "Thanks for the offer, but for me every day is Sunday. I say prayers all the time, right here." She spread her arms to indicate the room around her.

Later, as Jan concentrated on listening to mass, she thought about Willow's words. It seemed right to remember to be a little thankful all the time rather than make a big production once a week.

As they left the old stone church with its spectacular stained-glass windows, Jan tried not to think about how uncomfortable she'd been. She felt like she was wasting everyone's time — hers, Father Simpson's, and God's.

"Vi, can we stop at the office for a minute?" David nodded further up Lynx Street to the RCMP detachment. "There was a fourth poaching, and I have to pick up the ballistics report to see if it was the same rifle."

"Of course, but aren't you off today?" Her mom threw David a wry look.

David sighed. "I'm afraid I won't have much time off till we catch the creeps responsible. We have only about sixty grizzlies left in the park and they're being targeted. We lose enough bears to traffic accidents and railway hits without adding intentional harm." He hugged his bride. "Sorry, Violet."

"Hey, January, wait up!"

The familiar voice made Jan whirl around. It was Liam. "What are you doing here?" The minute the words were out of her mouth, she realized how dumb they sounded. "I mean, I haven't seen you here before."

Liam stuck his hands in his pockets. "I guess that's because we weren't teammates and chat-room buddies before."

Jan felt her face flame as both her mom and David looked at her for an explanation. She and Liam had discussed their project several times over the last week while in a chat room because Liam said he thought clearer in e-space. It had all been totally innocent, and the two-hour chats had nothing to do with the fact that Jan was starting to think Liam wasn't a bad guy at all, but rather a nice guy ... a cute, funny, smart, nice guy. But that's not the way it sounded and Jan knew it.

She put on what she hoped was a believable smile, dripping with innocence and nonchalance. "Mom, David, this is B. Liam Simpson, my computer project partner from school."

"Nice to meet you, Liam." Her mother smiled, warmly. "And nice to see Jan has made a new *friend*."

Jan wished they'd left ten minutes ago. "He's my project partner, Mom, that's all, nothing more." Jan thought she saw a flicker of something cross Liam's face. Had it been disappointment, or was he glad she'd made their business-only relationship so clear? "We have to go now, Liam. David has to stop at his office, you know, at work." She edged toward the street, desperately hoping her mom and David would follow. Jan didn't want to give her mom any more ammo for interrogation than she had to.

Liam took the hint. "Ah, right, see you at school tomorrow. Oh, I'd like to finish our splash page, so if you could get me the generic bear info you want included ASAP, I can put it together. Nice to meet you Mr. and Mrs. ..." He paused as though he didn't know how to refer to the couple, and Jan wished the ground would open up and swallow her.

57

"McKenna!" Jan's mom and David said at the same time, then both laughed.

"Nice to meet you, Mr. and Mrs. McKenna," Liam finished. Then, with shoulders hunched against the chilly breeze that had sprung up, he walked toward an old wreck of a car that Jan assumed was his.

"What a nice young man," Jan's mom said with only a little too much enthusiasm.

Jan didn't say anything.

* * *

When they arrived home, Willow was eating breakfast in the kitchen. Jan helped herself to a mug of coffee. "If you feel like taking in some sights today, we could add a few more dots to your map."

When Willow looked up quizzically, Jan noticed the dark circles around her eyes and wondered if more shut-eye wouldn't be a better idea. She remembered hearing Willow come in very late.

"What dots?"

"You know, on your computer map of sights to see."

"Oh, right." Willow reached into the pocket of her leather jacket slung over the back of her chair. "Sounds good. I have a couple of places I'd like to see." She placed a computer printout on the table.

Jan looked at the list. "Johnson's Canyon is a great hike, and Lake Louise and Morraine Lake are both super. We can do those too, but I had a spot in mind that will give you an idea of the country all around. How'd you like to go up the Sulphur Mountain gondola with me? The view from the top is spectacular, and we can go to the Banff Hot Springs and soak afterward."

"Let's go." Willow grabbed her coat and started for the door.

Jan laughed, pointing down at her long skirt. "Let me get out of this tent first." She gulped her coffee, then ran up to change into something more appropriate for a motorcycle ride.

* * *

The parking lot for the Sulphur Mountain gondola was so jammed with tourists they had to park at the Banff Upper Hot Springs and walk back. Jan started toward the admission gate, pulling her wallet out as she went.

Willow stopped her, pointing at a trail sign. "It says here we can walk up. It's a great day for a hike."

Jan looked at the trail sign, then at the towering mountain soaring over them. "Are you nuts? It will take freakin' hours!"

"Come on, Jan, it will be fun." Willow strode past the sign and disappeared into the forest beyond.

The sun was already warm and Jan stripped off her leather jacket. Climbing the mountain was insane, but if that's what Willow wanted, it was fine with her. With one last longing look at the waiting gondola, Jan started up the steep trail after Willow.

Two-and-a-half torturous hours later, they finally reached the top. Jan thought she was going to die. Her legs burned as the sweat ran down the inside of her leather motorcycle pants. The steep hike didn't seem to have fazed Willow, who was booking along at the same pace she'd started out with.

"Okay," Jan took a ragged breath and tried to ease the ache in her back, "that was way too tough for an out-of-shape teenager like me." She straightened up and looked around. "Oh, man!"

The view from the top was definitely worth the gruelling hike. The two young women stood staring at the panorama spread out before them. Neither spoke as they took in the 360-degree vista that stretched to the horizon, where snow-covered peaks glittered in the pristine mountain air.

"What a great place! My spirit guide feels at home here," Willow breathed appreciatively as she sat on a large boulder and continued to soak up the incredible scenery.

As Jan slumped down beside her, she noticed Willow wasn't out of breath or tired at all. The girl was incredibly fit!

"Your spirit guide?" Jan asked with a lift of one eyebrow.

Willow tossed a pebble over the embankment, and neither of them heard it hit bottom. "You know, the one who helps me. My grandfather told me to listen to both my heart and my spirit guide, and I would find my true path." She walked to the edge and peered over the precipice. "Banff rocks!"

As Jan bent over to pick up a stone, an excited squirrel shot out from under a juniper bush and scampered in front of her. The poor little guy had a misshapen ear and Jan wondered what owl had nearly had squirrel stew for its dinner. She laughed and held the rock out, waggling the chunk of limestone before she tossed it over the edge. "You mean like these?"

Willow groaned at Jan's pun, then picked up her jacket. "Okay, Shakespeare, let's start down."

"Wait a minute! I have to get something to eat before we go. I haven't had breakfast," she looked at her watch, "or lunch yet and I'm starved. There's a restaurant inside." She nodded at the building next to the gondola terminal.

"We can eat at home." Willow stood.

"Oh, no you don't! I'm not taking one step off this mountain until we refuel!" Jan started into the building and Willow reluctantly followed.

As they stood in line, Jan noticed Willow eyeing the pies in the display case. "Quit drooling and have a piece. On Sunday they're calorie-free!"

Willow looked uncomfortable. "Actually, they'd have to be *free,* period. I'm a little short on money at the moment."

Jan felt like an idiot. This was why Willow hadn't wanted to take the gondola up. She was broke and couldn't afford the admission fee! "Uh, actually, my mom gave me money for both of us to have a fun day," Jan lied. She had money from doing odd jobs around the neighbourhood, but knew Willow would feel better if she thought today was a total freebie for both of them. "She felt bad that she and David have been so busy they haven't had a chance to show you any of the sights themselves. So if everything's cool now, let's have that pie."

When Willow still hesitated, Jan reached into the cooler and took out two slices of banana cream pie and put them on the tray. "Don't make me eat these alone! Oh, by the way, if you hike up, the gondola ride down is free!"

Willow smiled in relief. "In that case, we ride in style!"

After lunch, Jan noticed her muscles were beginning to scream. "When we get to the bottom, I'm going to soak in the hot springs pool for the rest of my life." She thought of all the pins in Willow's map. "I'm sure the pool is on your list of attractions. After today's little jaunt, it's the perfect time to visit."

They rode the gondola down and it was like having a bird's-eye view of eternity. Jan shook her head. "Let's see, four-and-a-half-minute relaxing ride versus two-and-a-half-hour grinding hike! All because you were too shy to borrow a chunk of change! Truly bizarre." She turned toward the entrance to the Upper Hot Springs a short walk away. "Come on. No way am I missing this today!"

Willow didn't argue as Jan paid their way to the famous hot pool. The steaming mineral water felt wonderful on Jan's aching muscles and, as she soaked, she thought about Willow's words. "You said your spirit guide felt at home here. What's that mean exactly?" She closed her eyes and slid down into the hot water. The heat and strong mineral smell made her slightly dizzy.

Willow thought about her answer. "Spirit helpers are always out there, but sometimes we're so busy with ordinary things that we forget to invite them in." Willow slid Jan a sidelong glance. "Before we can see, we have to stop looking. I guess you could explain it by saying a spirit guide helps that inner voice we all have to make the right decision." She splashed the water with her hands, sending a cloud of scented vapour into the air. "I'm simply telling you what some think that voice is, and that we should accept the guidance offered."

Jan could understand this. "So I should pay more attention to my subconscious? You're saying that we already know the right thing to do, and we screw up when we don't listen?"

"It's not that simple. Sometimes we need extra help." Willow leaned back, gently fluttering her legs under the water.

"But I thought you said my spirit guide is inside me already?" Jan was confused.

"Good. You said '*my* spirit guide.' That means you acknowledge you have one, and that's an important step. You'll have to watch for signs so you'll know your guide when it shows up. I can help you with that."

Jan shook her head. This was getting crazy. "No, I didn't mean I believe in one, it's only a figure of speech." She didn't think such a thing as a spirit guide was real, but the idea of an outside force willing to help her find her way was appealing. Isn't that what the church told you? Say a Hail Mary, get help from Jesus' mom. She wondered if you prayed to your guide like you did to the saints in church. "Do you have to coax your spirit guide with prayers so he'll help you?" She thought of the countless rosaries she'd said in her life.

"First you have to find yours, talk to it, see how it wants to do things. Sometimes, if you have a lot of good in you, they're easy to get along with. But if you resist, they can be stubborn."

Jan thought she understood. "So if you're a bad person, they fight you."

"No."

Jan waited for more explanation, but Willow simply closed her eyes and turned her face up to the sunshine. Jan tried again. "When you say the spirit guide gets stubborn, you mean that if you resist by not believing in it, it will keep giving signs until you start to listen. That tells your guide you know it's there and you'll accept advice, because you believe it's real and want to do the right thing." Jan hoped she made sense.

Willow didn't open her eyes. "Closer. People call it intuition, coincidence, or luck, but often it's that crazy old spirit guide who helps you take the right turn."

"So only good people have a spirit guide?"

"We all put out energy, good and bad. It's when you continually send out bad energy that there's a problem. Bad attracts bad and there are other forces out there besides spirit guides."

"Like the *wittigo*?"

Willow bobbed her head. "Bad energy clouds our inner vision and we can't see the Sweetgrass Trail. We can wander lost a long time until we find it again. A spirit guide can help. Good energy binds together and links us. Being linked is good because that connection can never be severed, not even through death."

Jan sat up so suddenly she splashed water into her eyes. "What do you mean, 'not even through death?'"

"Just that. This link we are all part of goes on forever. Those who have gone to join our ancestors are still here for us." She paused, then looked directly into Jan's eyes. "For you."

Jan thought about a link that could never be cut off, never stopped. Willow said even someone who had died was still part of it, still here. Despite the heat of the water around her, a shiver ran through Jan. Long-forgotten images of her father pushing her on the swing in their backyard and carrying her on his broad shoulders flashed into her mind. What if what Willow said was true? It was a wonderful, wild way of looking at things.

Chapter 6

"If we could access the government information sites, we could get at some important data on the collared bears." It was Wednesday and Jan was at Liam's. She sighed as she re-read the meagre information she'd gathered since Sunday. By the time she and Willow had returned from the hot springs, it had been late and she hadn't been able to find the information Liam had wanted. Then, with practising for the race and a tedious math assignment due, the week had slipped away from her. Liam had been great and hadn't nagged her at all. When she talked to Mr. Dyer at Wapiti Trail Outfitters, he said he'd hunted all over Alberta and bears were the same everywhere, and he offered helpful advice on what to do if confronted by either a grizzly or a black bear. It was something, but not nearly enough.

Jan hoped to expand their site to trace the family trees of "their" bears back into the park's history.

She tossed her pen onto Liam's desk. "We need to start with the original collared bears, document how many cubs they had, and follow the family line for each bear up to the present day. But that's impossible because we can't access the right sites." The government didn't want hunters having information on where the sows are denning or where there was a high concentration of young bears. That would make hunting them too easy.

"That's not entirely true." Liam sat back in his chair. "It depends how badly you want in."

Jan stared at him, confused. "I'm talking about protected government sites."

"So am I." Liam let his sunglasses slip down his nose and arched his eyebrows at her.

"You're kidding, right?" Jan couldn't believe he meant what she thought he meant.

"Wizards never kid where cyberspace is involved. I have a reputation to uphold." Liam was deadly serious.

"I knew it!" she said. "You're one of those hackers, aren't you? One of those guys who build nasty viruses and break into top-secret web sites."

Liam gave her a shocked look. "I don't build *nasty* viruses," he said indignantly, then smiled. "In fact, I had the same idea as you, and have been working on cracking a couple of off-limit sites."

"No way. Liam, you can't do that! It's illegal. You could go to jail." Jan felt panic rising.

"Jan, calm down. I'm incredibly good at this. There's no way this hack can be traced back to my machine. I borrowed some government bit-head's identity, so this visit will never show up on their intrusion-detection systems. It will look like an employee is using the system from on-site. Besides, you need a good grade on this assignment and so do I. You're not the only one with dreams for the future."

Jan remembered their late-night online chat earlier that week, when she'd told Liam her plans to become a lawyer. He'd shared his own computer-dynasty dreams with her. They'd talked about which universities they were going to and how much money they'd owe when they finished their degrees. It was like she could tell him anything and he would understand. Jan had felt closer to Liam that night than any other person in the world.

Liam's fingers flew, then the screen blinked. "We're in!" His voice sounded confident and a little smug to Jan. "And we have lift-off …"

Jan was amazed and a little nervous. Liam had hacked into a restricted government site and was now navigating around like he owned the place. A page flashed up listing different Wildlife Management Units — WMUs — then Bear Management Areas within them. He accessed the files on grizzlies, then black bears. Images flashed and data scrolled down the screen.

"The files on bear sightings, population growth, and mortality in the park are perfect. Print those screens!" Jan said excitedly, then added in a calmer tone, "In case we can't get back in." Even if he said it was safe, she didn't think having Liam snoop on this site regularly was a good idea. Maybe the feds had some new way of detecting hackers no one knew about. Suddenly, a listing caught Jan's eye. "Stop!"

Liam's fingers froze. "What?"

"I want to have a look at the folder labelled *Poaching*."

"Sure." He smiled conspiratorially at her. "Jan, you're pumped! Don't deny it."

Jan looked back at him sheepishly, a tingle of guilty excitement lighting her eyes. "Are you going to open that folder or should I?" She held her index finger up in the air and wiggled it ominously.

Liam hit a key and, as she read the information on the screen, Jan was surprised at how little poaching had actually taken place in the park. In fact, this year's four incidents were already setting a record. She studied the map showing the kill sites. Banff was her hometown and it was freaky to think a cold-blooded poacher could be here among them. "Print this page too, please, Wiz."

Liam smiled at the use of his self-appointed title. "Hey, look at that!" he pointed to the spot in the centre of the map indicating where the first poaching had taken place. "It happened in Iron Rock Canyon. I've actually been there in the flesh. My brother, the pushy priest, dragged us out for a hike when we first got here. The dirt's as red as anything you'd find in Prince Edward Island!

Makes a real mess of white sneakers. They turn out a gross, girly shade of pink."

"Is there a manly shade of pink?" Jan teased as she studied the screen. Scanning the data, it came to her that she had access to a lot of insider info. An idea slid into her mind like it had been there all along. What if she could help David find the poacher? Now that she had temporary access to the government sites, she had almost as much information as David. Maybe she could spot something new, an overlooked clue that would bust the case wide open. There was only one catch. How could she ask David about it without him wondering where she got her information?

* * *

Jan waited nervously on the podium of the auditorium stage. It had been a scramble this past week, but today was the big day, the launch of her series *Extreme Careers — Do You Dare?* In an effort to look like a normal cookie-cutter high-school girl, she'd worn a cropped pastel-striped sweater and her new skirt, faded denim with a fringed hem. There wasn't much she could do with her short hair, but she'd applied a glittery peach lip gloss that tasted great.

David had agreed to wear his full-dress red serge and she could hardly wait. She would finally be a face the other kids associated with something totally awesome instead of being the new girl with the dark skin and bad hair.

Jan looked out at the assembled crowd. Ms. Glowinski, the principal, had decided the entire school should hear the speakers she'd arranged. The lineup for the series of talks was impressive. She had a smoke jumper who parachuted into wildfires to stop them, a deep-sea salvage diver, a woman test pilot for an aircraft manufacturer, an African safari photographer, and — to lead them all off — a Royal Canadian Mounted Police constable.

The series was a great idea. Liam had wished her luck and she'd dismissed him with assurance that luck wasn't necessary. But now, with everyone staring at her and murmuring impatiently, she wished it wasn't her neck on the block. She checked her watch for the hundredth time: 11:19.

Her stomach rumbled, reminding her she hadn't had breakfast. Where was this week's star speaker? Where was David? He was supposed to be here twenty minutes ago. He hadn't sent a message saying he couldn't make it. She'd phoned the detachment, but they didn't know where he was.

The assembly looked like a mob of prison inmates ready to riot, and Jan wished she wasn't the only person on the stage. As Ms. Glowinski walked toward her, the lava churning in Jan's stomach threatened to erupt.

"January, I'm sorry, I'm going to have to dismiss the students." The principal's face was stern.

"I don't know what happened to him. He knew he was supposed to speak this morning." Jan had the sinking feeling David had forgotten.

The auditorium door opened and Jan saw Willow walk in and stand quietly at the back; her arms folded like a prison guard. Perfect! What every riot needed — official crowd control.

A desperate idea hit Jan. Maybe she could save both the program and her own skin! She tapped the microphone for everyone's attention, but before she could say anything, a loud growl, reminiscent of a hungry grizzly, echoed throughout the gym. Too late, she realized the mic was on and had picked up her complaining stomach, broadcasting her distress to the waiting crowd.

Everyone burst out laughing and a couple of students offered rude comments. Jan cringed and wished she were on a plane to anywhere. Instead, she took a deep breath and introduced her first guest speaker to the restless crowd.

"Ladies and gentlemen, I would like to introduce Willow Whitecloud, who is in the Royal Canadian Mounted Police Summer Student Program." Jan frantically waved at Willow.

Willow hesitated at hearing her own name. Then, as she looked around and noticed Constable McKenna was nowhere in sight, understanding broke across her face. With a wave to the crowd, Willow strode confidently up the centre aisle and leapt onto the stage.

"Good morning," she began. "My name is Willow Whitecloud and I am proud to say I am a supernumerary summer student. That unpronounceable mouthful is my official designation as a member of the RCMP Summer Student Program, which allows young people to experience what real policing is like first-hand."

Jan felt the knot in her stomach begin to ease as the crowd focused on Willow.

"I must admit, as I walked up that aisle just now, I felt a little like the one who was voted off the island — singled out and sent to my doom." Willow smiled winningly as she shot Jan a you-owe-me-big-time glance. A ripple of laughter went through the audience, who seemed to enjoy Willow's easy style. "From the hundreds of applicants, only thirty-five were chosen for K-Division and seven for the national program this year. To even be in the running, you have to be at least eighteen, with a high-school diploma. For the national, you also have to be enrolled in a university or college — so don't quit your day jobs."

Another burst of laughter. Jan loved it. This was going great!

Willow went on. "I'm nineteen and taking a course from Northern Lights College to become a First Nations Human Services Worker, so I fit the bill."

The audience listened raptly as Willow went on about the training and some of the exciting experiences she'd had on the job. The students thought it was cool that Willow wore an RCMP uniform, even without the firearm.

Jan had started to feel good about the way the talk was going when something Willow said made her head snap up.

"And I will ultimately be a shaman for my band. First Nations peoples have a strong bond with the land and the spirits that move across it. As shaman, I would help others communicate with those spirits and help them walk the Sweetgrass Trail."

Jan sat bolt upright in her chair. This was not what she wanted these kids to hear. Willow could come off sounding like a freak if you didn't understand her deeply traditional roots, and Jan didn't want to be remembered as the one who brought the soothsayer in on career day.

Still, as Willow went on to explain how, as a shaman, she would heal people using natural medicines known for hundreds of years, Jan was intrigued. Willow made it sound perfectly natural, like going to medical school or being a parish priest.

How her fellow students would take this turn in the presentation was anyone's guess, but one thing was for certain: if David had shown up, Jan wouldn't have had to worry about any of this. The knot in her stomach came back with a vengeance. How could David have forgotten? This program was *only* the biggest thing Jan had ever done.

When Willow ended her talk, the audience sat in stunned silence. Jan had been wondering about audience reception, and here was her answer. Hearing about the RCMP Summer Student Program, great; having to sit through an infomercial about shamanism, not so much. She jumped to her feet. "Thank you, S.S. Whitecloud. That was …" she smiled weakly, "enlightening."

74

The whispers and nervous giggles started immediately and Jan winced. They were not the kind of whispers or giggles that signalled a rousing success. The prisoners filed out.

Liam waited until the grumbling crowd left, then walked up to the stage to join Willow and Jan.

"That went well," he grinned up at Jan.

"Yeah, no one threw anything." She looked from Liam to Willow. "No one can ever accuse you of being a boring speaker!"

"Hey, I saved your butt!" Willow protested. "I may have gotten a little off topic, but they seemed to like it."

"Oh, they'll never forget it!" Jan laughed.

"Come on," Willow climbed down off the stage. "I'll buy you two lunch."

"Ah, I really shouldn't," Liam protested. "I brought a brown bag."

Jan knew the hard-core hard-drive freak would sit in front of a terminal in the computer lab his entire lunch, hacking or playing some weird game with contestants from around the globe. "So? Believe it or not, B. Liam Simpson, interacting in real space is more fun than in e-space. You can feed your gourmet pb and j to the squirrels. We're celebrating my near escape from a tar and feathering."

Jan and Willow started out into the noon sunshine as Liam reluctantly followed. To Jan's surprise, they went to a very good and very expensive restaurant on Banff Avenue.

Liam hesitated. "Are you sure you want to go

here?" He looked at the gold lettering over the elaborately carved wooden door.

"Willow, this is an uber-pricey place. We can go somewhere cheaper. I'm not that broken up about being ditched by my stepfather on the most important day of my school life." Jan couldn't help the bitter note in her voice. She was angry, but managed to shove it aside.

"Jeez, sounds like you need a good meal, Jan. Don't worry, I've got it covered." Willow pushed the ornate door open and led the way in.

The conversation consisted of Jan and Willow talking about the grizzly poaching while Liam sat like a lump. "Cheer up, Wiz. You can get your computer fix later. Besides, some of your cyber-buddies must live in time zones where it's past their bedtime. Let them sleep." They were sitting beside each other on a leather banquette and she bumped him with her shoulder. "Things could be worse. You could be me, the girl who almost got the entire school body assembled for nothing. Thank goodness Willow was here to bail me out."

Willow finished her iced tea and smiled at Jan. "I guess your first speaker wasn't what you expected." She turned to Liam "So what does your dad do?"

"He leaves." Liam said without missing a beat.

Willow looked at him blankly and Jan jumped in. "Liam's dad and mom are divorced."

Willow nodded. "Divorce is kind of like death." She turned to Jan. "Those left behind always feel guilty in some way."

76

Jan suddenly felt sick, her stomach tense. "Can we change the subject?" she blurted out loudly, causing the other diners to stop and stare at them.

Startled, Willow and Liam immediately did as she asked. Willow brought up the subject of the latest computer games and Liam dived into a topic that was near and dear to his heart. Before long he and Willow were arguing animatedly over the merits of the latest hot game from Japan. Jan stared at the filigree pattern on her empty plate and didn't say another word.

By the time they finished lunch, Jan's tension had started to ease. Then her thoughts returned to the speaker fiasco, and that caused her full stomach to churn again. "Isn't there some way I can skip afternoon classes? Willow, can't you arrange a three-alarm emergency to clear the building?" she asked, only half joking.

"Hey I'm good, but I'm not a miracle worker!" Willow laughed as she left the server a very generous tip.

Liam raised an eyebrow. "Wow, when I get a job as a waiter, I hope you come to my restaurant!"

Jan didn't say anything, but she wondered how Willow had suddenly come into so much money.

Chapter 7

Jan slammed the back door.

Her stepdad was at work in his den and Jan decided to give him a piece of her mind. But when she walked in, all she could think about was making things better so there'd be no fight. "Uh, David, today was the day you were supposed to speak to the assembly at school." He looked up and his face blanched. She waved her hand nonchalantly. "No biggie, really. I had another speaker come in. No sweat."

"Oh, my God. Jan, I am so sorry! It completely slipped my mind." He rubbed his tired eyes. "The poacher struck again, near the east park gates. We still don't have any clues except for the calibre of the bullet and the fact that, again, only the paws and gall bladder were harvested."

His haggard face made Jan want to re-double her efforts to help find the poacher. She choked back her anger. From the way David looked, he was willing to work himself into the ground until he caught whoever was responsible. "It's okay. Maybe next time." Getting mad at David wouldn't do any good. It was her fault anyway. He was busy. She should have reminded him, left messages at work and at home. She went to her room before she used up all the grown-up self-control she was throwing around.

Sitting at her desk, Jan booted up her computer. She'd promised Liam she'd get the information for their splash page to him today. They'd decided their home page would have general information on grizzlies so visitors could get an overview of the big bears. Jan connected to the Internet and accessed a public site titled *Grizzlies of Banff National Park*. It had lots of excellent pictures and she wondered if they could import some to their web page.

She read that the grizzlies in Banff kept their twin cubs with them for up to five years, which was a much longer nurturing period than black bears had. They didn't start reproducing until they were over five years old, which meant that one bear's lifetime of twenty-five years didn't produce many offspring to fill the gaps created by bears lost from human contact. The park had put up fences to keep the animals off the roads, and built wildlife corridors so they could get from one side to the other. Despite these precautions, cars still hit bears, and the animals had no protection from the freight trains that roared through day and night.

Opening their web page, Jan looked at the list of collared bears she and Liam were following. Her favourite was Number 66, a twenty-year-old sow that had been around Banff for years and had had a lot of cubs. Jan smiled at how well Number 66 had done in trying to build the population. She'd had two litters of three cubs each and a set of twins.

Without warning, a pop-up ad filled the screen with dancing pill bottles advertising cheap rates for prescription drugs. With a groan, Jan watched as the bottles stopped dancing, her cursor stopped blinking, and her screen faded to the dreaded blue. She tried unsuccessfully to reboot her computer, but it was having some kind of meltdown and wouldn't respond to her commands, giving her an undecipherable error message instead. Perfect!

Jan cursed the cruel gods of cyberspace, then remembered Willow had a laptop in her room. She didn't think S.S. Whitecloud would mind if she used the machine for a few minutes to finish her research. Hurrying to Willow's room, Jan turned on the computer. As she waited for the usual buzzes and clicks signalling a connection being made to the Internet, she noticed Willow had a folder marked *Grizzly* listed on her hard drive. It was clear that she was doing research too. Maybe they could share data.

Jan hesitated, her finger poised over the mouse. Snooping in someone's computer was like reading a diary, but she was going to look at only the bear folder, not Willow's personal correspondence or e-mails. She clicked the folder tab and a list of files winked onto the screen.

As Jan read the list, she began to wonder if she should stop. They looked like official Alberta Fish and Wildlife files. The girl must really want to do a good job if she was bringing work home. Two files caught Jan's eye, *Bear Licences — Drawn Names* and *Bear Licences — Substituted Names.* She clicked on the one marked *Drawn Names*, but the file wouldn't open. Instead a message box came up, telling her the file was password protected. She tried *Substituted Names* but it was the same. A familiar rumble from the driveway alerted her that Willow was home.

Jan felt a blush of guilt at her attempted cyber break-and-enter, and decided she must have caught some kind of hacking bug from Liam. As she quickly shut down the laptop, it struck Jan as odd that Willow would have these files in her own computer, even password protected.

She scurried to her room and was lying on her bed when Willow walked past. "Hi, I was thinking of going for a ride later. Want to come?" Jan sounded casual.

"Sure," Willow agreed. "I'll be back in an hour. I have to zip to the detachment first."

Willow retrieved a notebook from her room and had started back down the narrow steps that led to the kitchen, when Jan remembered she had not finished her homework for B. Liam Simpson, computer tyrant. "Hey, my computer's down. Can I use yours to access the Net?" she called out.

Willow hesitated. "Uh, my Internet connection is down too. Why don't you call Liam and see if his is working?"

Jan opened her mouth, then closed it. What could she say? That Willow was mistaken because Jan had just been on her machine and it worked fine? "No worries. It will probably be back up later."

After Willow left, Jan went to the kitchen to make coffee. She remembered that David was working in his den and took him a cup. "How's it going?" she asked as she nudged a set of handcuffs aside to set the coffee down. A red light flashed on the fax machine. "Is the fax broken?" Picking a faintly printed page out of the hopper, Jan squinted but was unable to read the ghostly words.

"No, the cartridge is nearly done. I hope no one's tried to send me a fax. I meant to pick up a new one but I've been so busy …" He took the coffee. "Thanks. And as far as how the job's coming, well, *slowly* might be a word I'd use, or maybe *dead in the water*. All we know for sure is that the bears were all killed with the same rifle." David sipped his scalding brew.

Jan dropped the paper back into the fax tray. She felt a little guilty about breaking into Willow's computer and wondered if she could make up for it by getting their boarder a gold star with David. "It's a good thing Willow's here. She really wants to help. I think she brings work home. That's got to be above and beyond the call of duty, right?"

"Actually, bringing files home is against the rules for a summer student." David arched his back, stretching. "Sometimes new officers don't understand what's sensitive material and what's okay for the general public to know. By keeping everything at work, there's no worry about information falling into the wrong hands."

"What about computer work? She could have files in her computer to work on if they were password protected, right?" Jan knew she was pushing it but she wanted to show Willow as a star.

"Same thing. Absolutely no computer files leave the office at any time. Even protected files can be hacked into. Civilians don't have the security on their home units that we have at the detachment." David motioned to the array of paperwork on his desk. "Security is important, Jan. I always lock these up in my desk drawer if I have to leave the house. Also, the poaching case is special and requires me to bring work home. It has long hours and lots of overtime." He smiled ruefully. "Both the long hours and the overtime put in by yours truly."

Jan glanced at her watch. "Rats! I'm supposed to finish an important chunk of our computer project and e-mail it to Liam! Later!" She hurried out of the room. Her plan to highlight Willow's good deeds hadn't turned out the way she'd hoped. In fact, from what David had said, Willow might be heading for big trouble.

Chapter 8

A half-hour later, Jan was still wondering how to tell Willow to stop bringing work home without letting on how she knew work had been brought home, when the sound of a motorcycle pulling into their driveway signalled it was time for their ride. Jan grabbed her gear and met Willow outside. "Where do you want to go?" she asked as she jerked her helmet down and buckled the chinstrap.

"I've got something really cool — no, really *hot* — in mind." Willow said mysteriously. "Follow me."

They travelled out of Banff National Park, then turned east onto the 1-A highway at Canmore. After a while, Jan realized they were on the Stoney First Nation lands; she'd been to pow-wows there with her mom. Finally, Willow stopped in a small parking area under some trees. Climbing off her bike, she pulled a bundle out of her tank bag and started striding across the tall prairie grass.

"Where are we going?" Jan asked, following behind. Through the trees ahead she spotted smoke. As they moved closer, she saw a young man tending a fire in which a pile of rocks glowed red-hot. Beside the fire was a domed hut about the height of a man. It was made of willow branches covered with animal hides. Jan eyed the strange structure. "Or should that be, what are we doing?"

When they arrived at the clearing, an ancient First Nations elder with long iron-gray braids met them. Willow and the elder spoke, then Willow nodded and turned to Jan, handing her a bundle of cloth. "Jan, this is Mr. Black Elk. He'll lead the sweat this afternoon."

Jan felt her jaw drop. Had she heard right? "Hello, sir." Hesitantly, she nodded a greeting before following Willow toward a clump of bushes with a bench hidden discreetly behind.

"Willow," she whispered frantically. "That gentleman is going to lead a *what?*" Although her mother had talked about sweat lodges before, Jan had never actually done a sweat.

"After we climbed Sulphur Mountain, you took me to the hot springs and we soaked until we were healed from the ordeal. Today, we will experience my version of soaking and healing — a traditional sweat. It's not a women's sweat, but we've been welcomed into this one. Willow indicated toward the bundle. "That's a long cotton nightgown you need to change into. Oh, and take off any metal jewellery you might be wearing. It's going to get hot in there."

Jan didn't know what to say. She silently followed Willow's lead.

They entered the sweat lodge and sat to the left of the hide-covered door. Coloured cloths and figures of animals decorated the interior walls. A pile of superheated rocks nestled in a depression in the centre of the grass-covered floor and a wave of hot air immediately assailed Jan's lungs. Several men of various ages and wearing very little clothing filled in the remaining spaces around the fire pit.

The elder Willow had introduced as Mr. Black Elk told a young man who waited at the door to bring in the remaining rock, the white one, and seal the lodge. He did as he was instructed and the sweat lodge was immediately plunged into darkness. The grey-haired gentleman passed a long pipe around to the other men, but did not offer it to Jan and Willow, the only two women present.

The elder began to chant in a language Jan didn't understand as he threw herbs onto the rocks, then poured water over them with a wooden ladle. The stones hissed and sang as fragrant steam rose, filling the dark lodge. Jan smelled sweetgrass, cedar, and sage. Her senses began to drift with the clouds of steam. The heat was overwhelming.

The elder explained that this sweat was to send prayers to the Creator to help Anthony Dodginghorse, who was gravely ill and not expected to live through the day.

Willow leaned over and whispered, "You should offer this sweat up to someone you want to help, or someone you want to remember and make peace with."

Jan looked at her, but couldn't speak.

The elder sang, the soft notes carrying Jan with them as they rose and fell. The old man said a final prayer as he poured water on the hot stones, then the hide door to the lodge was thrown open.

"Wow! That was incredible!" Jan pushed her sweaty hair back off her forehead. "I thought I was going to melt."

"We'll have three more rounds before we're through. Can you take it?" Willow asked, concern in her voice.

Jan looked at her in surprise. "Three more, huh? I thought this one par-boil was it." She took a deep drink from the water bottle that was being passed around. "You know, once you accept being in a tanned-hide pressure cooker, it's actually very pleasant." She took a deep breath of air still heavy with moisture.

"The lodge is like being inside the skin of a great animal, with the covering being the night sky above your head." Willow explained. "It's a place of power and healing."

"You talked about my spirit helper and putting out good energy so I would be linked to all the other good out there." Jan didn't know how to phrase what she wanted to ask. "And you mentioned I should offer this sweat up to someone I want to make peace with. Do you really believe that can happen?"

Willow turned her dark eyes to Jan and, through some trick of the light, they looked like they were lit from within. "The question is, Jan, do you believe it can happen?"

The elder waved his hand and the doorway was sealed again. The sweat continued and the heat was even more intense than it was before. Jan thought of her dead father and her face grew wet with tears.

After the sweat was completed, Willow gave Mr. Black Elk a pouch of tobacco and thanked him for allowing them to participate. When it came time for Jan to thank the elder, he spoke softly to her in a language she couldn't understand, and smiled in a way that made her feel completely at peace.

A large squirrel ran in front of Jan as she walked slowly back to her motorcycle through the tall grass. The sweat had been an incredible experience, almost other-worldly. A piercing shriek from overhead made her look up. Shielding her eyes against the late-afternoon sun, she saw a large golden eagle circling above. The eagle followed Jan and Willow to where they'd parked. With one last plaintive cry, it flew away.

Willow watched the tiny speck recede into the far distance. "Mr. Black Elk told me he just received word that Mr. Dodginghorse has had a good turn. He's getting better." She pulled her helmet on and started her bike.

* * *

Monday, Jan stopped Liam in the hallway. She'd tried a new hairstyle, but the gel made it so stiff that, when she turned her head, it felt like she had a motorcycle helmet on. She also wore plum-coloured eye shadow and the lipgloss from the disastrous assembly, but kept having to remind herself not to lick off the tasty goop. She hoped Liam would like her makeover. "My computer refuses to resurrect itself from the dead. I need your magic touch. Can you have a look?"

Liam shifted his backpack and stared at her hair. "You have a corkscrew of hair sticking straight up like an antenna. Is that the look you were going for?"

Jan touched her hair and groaned inwardly. How long had she walked around with a hair spike sticking out of her head? Hastily, she smoothed the crusty hair flat. "I thought I'd try something different," she said coolly. "What about my computer, will you help?"

"Actually, I'm busy after school. But if you can get the hard drive over to my house, I could trouble-shoot it there."

Jan stared at him incredulously. "You're kidding, right? Tear my hard drive apart when it could be a simple wrong connection or bad command from the server! What about later? Could you stop by then?" Jan knew he was thinking about spending a leisurely afternoon and evening surfing the web, but this was the real world and she needed his help. "What's that matter? Don't you want to come over to my house?"

"No, it's not that. It's well, I …" Liam's voice trailed off.

"I know you don't like being away from the bat cave, but I need help. Couldn't you please come over for five minutes?" she wheedled. "I promise I won't bite." She could see he was about to turn her down again. She reached out and touched his arm. "Pretty please with floppy disks on top."

With a smile, Liam relented. "Okay. I'll be there at four." He turned to leave, then stopped. "And only if you wash that axle grease out of your hair. I like the way you look without all that gunk the other girls pour on. Some of those divas use so much hairspray, they're a fire hazard."

Jan watched him walk away and suddenly felt like humming.

He arrived exactly at four and, without a word, followed Jan to her room. After checking several settings and programs, he diagnosed the problem as being "deep within the brain of the beast."

Jan watched him work. "It's those stupid pop-ups. I wish I could send an e-bomb back to the jerks who built them and melt their cyber-brains."

"I blew off a serious game of D and D for this. It looks like you may have had a Trojan sneak in with this lame ad. Now I'm really ticked." He quickly hit several keys, but the ad remained. Cursing, he ran his hand through his thick blond hair. "This is stupid. It's going to take a dog's age to ferret the skunk out." He keyed in a series of new commands.

Jan would have smiled at his dopey animal analogy, but could see Liam was genuinely upset. If she didn't know better, she'd say he was seriously preoccupied with something other than computers. She'd never seen him like this. Not wanting to spook him any further, she sat on her bed and looked at the data on the printouts. "Can I get you something to drink?" she offered.

"No," he snapped, then sighed. "Look, I'm sorry to be such a pain."

"You think?" Jan realized she wasn't being a very good friend and changed her tone. "Hey, it's okay. I understand," she said sympathetically.

He avoided her gaze. "I heard from my dad. He's moving ... and not across town." He threw a pencil onto the desk. "He's going to Australia — the other end of the freakin' Earth."

"Oh, Liam, that so sucks. I'm sorry. But think how it will rock when you visit him on vacation." Jan offered helpfully.

"Yeah, except it costs two grand for a ticket. Oh, and one other little bombshell he dropped — my dad is marrying some bimbo he met down there." Liam looked at her and Jan saw real pain in his pale blue eyes. "They're 'starting over fresh,' he says, as if being with my mom was some kind of terrible mistake and I don't count. It's like once he leaves, he never has to deal with us again. We'll be dead to him!" His voice was loud in the small room.

Jan's hands started to tremble. She opened her

mouth to say something, but no words came out.

Liam stopped and looked at her. "Oh, crap. I'm sorry, Jan; I shouldn't have said that. I'm such a loser. I know you miss your dad a lot."

Jan swallowed, then tried to smile, but couldn't pull it off. "It's okay, forget it. Look, a computer genius like you could use a web cam and mic. You don't have to lose touch." Her voice broke.

Liam came over to sit beside her on the bed. "You're right." He gave her a half smile. "When life hands you lemons, go to the mall, or some stupid thing like that."

"Some stupid thing," she agreed. Jan wanted to change the subject. She didn't know what had come over her. "I have to check some data on the Internet. Willow's hooked up. I'll ask if we can use her computer for an hour." Since the extraordinary sweat, Jan hadn't had a chance to talk to Willow. She got up and went to find her.

The experience in the sweat lodge had made Jan think about things she hadn't allowed into her brain for a long time. Although it made the ache in her heart come back, she'd done as Willow suggested and offered up her sweat to her dad's memory. Sitting in the darkened lodge, breathing in the steamy sweetgrass-scented air, she remembered the day of the accident. The guilt had made the tears come. Jan still hadn't decided whether the whole sweat lodge experience had been totally good or spectacularly bad.

Willow wasn't in the kitchen or living room.

When Jan checked the driveway, she saw that her bike was gone. "Well, this bites!" she fumed, her research thwarted again. It was as if the universe was conspiring against her. Jan decided Willow wouldn't mind if her computer was borrowed once more. She promised herself that she wouldn't open any files she shouldn't.

Just as she started upstairs, the back door opened and her mother came into the kitchen.

"Hello, Honey." Her mother kicked off her shoes. "Whew, what a day. I'm beat."

"Hi, Mom. Liam and I are working on my computer. I'll be done in an hour and I can help with supper then."

"That would be great." Her mom put her bag down on the table. " I'll take a couple of steaks out of the freezer. With everyone rushing around, we've been eating poorly lately. It's time for a few green leafy vegetables."

"I can make a Caesar salad. And maybe we should have an early night. With all the overtime, I'm worried David's getting overdrawn at the sleep bank."

Her mom quirked an eyebrow. "My, aren't you the little mother hen."

"Later." Jan gave her mom a quick peck on the cheek and retreated up the narrow staircase.

After checking out three bear information sites, Jan shut down Willow's computer without so much as a peek at any of the other files. She felt vindicated for the earlier breach of computer etiquette.

There was a sudden banging and cursing from

downstairs. Jan and Liam ran to see what was going on. Jan's mom, now in jeans and a T-shirt, had her head and shoulders stuck in a cabinet under the bathroom sink. Water sprayed out in all directions.

"What can we do?" Jan tossed towels down to soak up the flood.

"Hand me a pipe wrench." Her mom stuck her hand out from inside the cupboard.

Liam hurried to the toolbox her mom had open on the floor and rummaged until he found the right tool. "Here you are, Mrs. McKenna."

Jan's mom beat on the pipe. There was a loud bang and then a fresh torrent of water spewed out. Her mother began using language Jan didn't realize she even knew. The bathroom floor was covered in water that was running into the hall.

"Where's the main shut-off valve?" Liam yelled, his sneakers submerged in the flooding tide.

"In the basement, beside the washing machine. Jan, show him!" Her mother tried to wrap a towel around the broken pipe to stop the geyser.

Quickly, Jan took Liam downstairs into the basement where he located the valve and screwed it shut. The sound of running water stopped. "Wow. That was close." Liam grinned at her. "I thought I was going to have to build us an ark, and I'm not good with power tools!"

They hurried back upstairs, grabbing extra towels on the way. Together, they mopped up the water, and had just finished wringing out the last towel when David walked into the room.

"What happened?" he asked, surveying the soggy mess.

Jan's mom swept her wet hair back off her forehead. "I was sick of the dripping pipe, so I thought I'd fix it, but the rusty thing broke and, well ..." She looked around at the damp bathroom.

"Why didn't you leave it for me?" David took the wet towels from Jan and Liam.

"Because, my dear husband," Jan's mom began, "you have enough to do with the poaching. Besides, I've fixed leaky pipes before. It would have been okay except the pipe was rust-weakened."

David smiled at Jan and Liam. "I think we should go for a hamburger break. We could all use dry clothes. I can pick up some plumbing supplies on the way and take care of this when we get back."

Jan's mom squeezed water out of the hem of her shirt. "I'll put the steaks back in the freezer."

Jan didn't want to inflict this torture on Liam. An hour in a restaurant with her mom and the burgers wouldn't be the only thing grilled. "Uh, we have to finish our homework. I'll make grilled cheese for Liam and me."

Her mom leaned against David, leaving a dampened patch on his shirt. "Okay. But I have to warn you, Liam, Jan's idea of gourmet cooking is to put dill pickles in her grilled cheese!"

Liam took his sunglasses off his head and tucked them into his shirt pocket. "Actually, Mrs. McKenna, I'm not bad in the kitchen. If I can track down a handful of bacon bits and a little

95

onion, I make a mean pasta Alfredo."

Jan stared at him, speechless. The guy could cook, too!

"That makes me feel much better. Jan's great at a lot of things, but she hasn't quite mastered the finer details of the kitchen," her mother teased.

Jan was now frowning so hard her eyebrows hurt.

"But she is good with a can opener and a microwave," David added in his stepdaughter's defence.

Jan cringed. Were parents given a manual on how to embarrass their kids or was it a talent they were born with? She looked down at the soggy floor, hoping a hole would open up that she could dive into.

"Okay, you two go out, and *Chef boy*-r-dee here," she jerked her thumb at Liam, "and I will muddle through somehow!" Studiously avoiding her computer partner's smiling face, Jan grabbed the wet towels from David and started downstairs to dump them in the washing machine.

* * *

Thursday night, as Jan sat in front of the TV, Grey called to say he'd finished prepping the bike. "I think the bike's as ready as it's ever going to be. The question, is what about the pilot? You up for Sunday?" Grey pressed.

Jan couldn't believe time had flown past so quickly. It had been nearly a month since Willow had come to stay with them, the poaching had started, and she'd met B. Liam Simpson. Now it was almost race day, when everything would be on the line — all Grey's dreams and her hopes for him. "I'm so pumped, I can hardly sleep!"

"Try to get as much rest as possible. I don't want you over-practising and peaking too soon. You're ready for this, Jan. I know you'll do great."

Jan could hear the confidence in her brother's voice and she vowed not to let him down. As she hung up the phone, a noise from David's study made her ears perk up. David and her mom were both working late. Quietly, Jan walked into the hall that led to the small den. A thin slice of light showed beneath the door. The hairs prickling on the back of her neck made her feel something was wrong or, she thought ruefully, maybe it was her spirit guide telling her to head for the hills!

As she edged down the dark hallway, the deep shadows closed around her like wings around the body of a bat. Jan stood in front of the study door, listening, then slowly reached out her hand. Just as her fingertips touched the knob, the door was jerked open.

Chapter 9

"What were you doing in there?" Jan's voice was somewhere between a squeak and a shriek.

Willow stared back as though looking for the right words. "I, I had to use the fax machine to make copies of a report I'm working on."

Jan exhaled the breath she'd been holding. "You may as well shoot me as scare me to death! I practically had heart failure."

Willow brushed past her and headed for the kitchen. "Sorry about the adrenaline rush, Jan. I'd better get back to it."

As Willow left, Jan looked into her stepdad's study. Everything seemed normal. She walked over to the fax machine. A sheet of paper still lay in the tray. Willow must have forgotten one of her pages. As Jan reached to pick it up, she noticed a red light blinking. The paper in her hand was the same faintly printed page she'd seen days ago. The blinking light meant David still hadn't replaced the cartridge. No faxes or copies could have been made on this machine.

A crease furrowed Jan's forehead. She tried the drawer where her stepdad stored his work papers. It was still locked. If Willow had been trying to snoop in that drawer, she would have been unsuccessful. But why would she do that? Was she spying on the poacher investigation?

That made no sense. Why didn't she simply ask David?

*   *   *

Friday afternoon, Jan was stretched out on her bed listening to her MP3 player when Willow breezed past her room. "Hey, Willow, I'm going to confession later. You could come and wait for me, then we could go for a ride."

Willow's tone was as serious as the grave. "Confession? What does a girl like you have to confess? Last time I checked, your only sin was your cooking, and I don't think God would hold that against you."

Jan was taken aback. "Nothing big, I guess, but it's something I've always done. You don't have to be an axe murderer to go to confession. But if you were, you probably should," she added with a smile.

"You're a good person, Jan. I can see it and I can feel it. The Creator wants his children to work on being good, not worry about being bad. I don't see how sitting in a dark closet trying to remember if you took the Lord's name in vain five times or six is going to make you a better person." Willow leaned against the door jam as if waiting for Jan to justify something she'd never given much thought to before.

"It's not that trivial," Jan said defensively. "It's part of staying in touch with ourselves, with God. It makes you think before you do something wrong."

Willow shook her head. "So if you didn't do this soul purge once a week, you'd rush out and rip off the local corner store?"

"Of course not." Jan sat up and folded her legs under her.

"And by confessing, it wipes the bad stuff out and you earn a get-out-of-hell-free card. Tell me, is there a scale for penance?"

Jan was confused. "A scale?"

Willow smiled. "Yeah, you know — three Hail Marys for taking a candy bar, ten Our Fathers for kicking a cat. And what about banking points for good behaviour? Can you store up penance to be used for a later sin?"

Jan tried not to giggle. "Not that I'm aware of. Maybe I'll check with Father Simpson today and get back to you."

Willow straightened. "It's all too complicated for a simple girl from the bush like me to understand. I'm going out for a while." She started to leave, then stopped. "I almost forgot. I was thinking that, since the race is Sunday, an exciting ride

100

in a cop car early Saturday morning might help to settle your nerves. What do you say to a ride-along tomorrow?"

Jan thought this was an entirely brilliant idea. "I'd like that. Grey says I'm supposed to rest so I can totally kick at the race, but a girl could use a little diversion to calm her heaving stomach."

"Great! I'll set it up with my partner." Willow waved and left, humming as she bounded down the stairs.

Jan thought about Willow after she left. She had some radical and irreverent ways of looking at things, especially spiritual things. The only problem was, Jan had wondered some of those very same things herself.

* * *

Saturday morning, Jan sat in the back of the RCMP patrol car, not believing she was going on a ride-along with Willow and Corporal Sloan. Okay, it was more of a jaunt from Lynx Street to Bow Falls, but it was exciting anyway. It was weird to be sitting in a police car again. She remembered riding to the hospital in David's patrol car after Grey's accident. That hadn't been fun at all.

She was in the back seat where the prisoners rode and it gave her a creepy feeling! There was a clear acrylic divider called a *silent patrolman* that separated her from Willow and Corporal Sloan. All the electronic gadgetry was hooked up in the front and, as Jan scanned the dash and console, she saw there was a lot more than a radar device for catching speeders. Jan shivered; she knew there was also a loaded shotgun in the car. Looking up, she was astonished to see footprints across the inside of the roof.

"Have you made much headway in the poacher case?" Willow asked Corporal Sloan as they pulled out on the street and turned toward Banff Avenue. "I haven't talked to David in days and was wondering if anything new is breaking."

Since finding Willow in David's study under suspicious circumstances, Jan had viewed Willow in an altered light, one that made her feel slightly uncomfortable.

Sloan moved closer to the car ahead of them. "Working on it. David's got a couple of leads he's checking out."

"I was thinking of talking to Dyer again to find out if he's heard any rumours, or if anyone's been asking for information on grizzly sightings." Willow looked at her supervisor. "It might help and I don't mind doing it."

The burly cop gave her a sidelong glance. "I think you should leave that to the officers assigned. In fact, I'll check out Dyer myself."

Jan saw something flash across Willow's face. Was it anger? Yes, Willow didn't like the idea of her involvement being curtailed.

Sloan nodded at the car ahead of them. "Run a 10-29 on that black Subaru. The plate's expired and it's out of province." He reached down to the console and hit a switch activating the light bar on the roof, flipped on the wigwag headlights, and blipped the siren. The black car immediately pulled over to the side of the road.

Willow keyed in the licence-plate number on the laptop computer sitting between the front seats. "The RO is Kenneth Johnson of Saskatoon."

"What's an RO?" Jan asked, intrigued by the specialized cop-code.

"Registered owner." Willow pulled her peak cap on.

Sloan settled his hat on his bush of hair. "Let's go chat with Mr. Johnson." He looked at his partner. "Ready?"

"Ready." Willow climbed out of the car.

Jan was fascinated and suddenly a little nervous as she waited while Sloan and S.S. Whitecloud performed actual RCMP duties. She watched the mini-drama unfold as Corporal Sloan walked up to the driver's door of the black Subaru. As he did this, Willow approached the opposite side of the car, stopping at the back doors.

Sloan spoke to the driver, who handed him what Jan assumed was his driver's licence and registration. Sloan checked the documents carefully and wrote the driver a summons before handing back the papers. This finished, he and Willow returned to the police car as the tourist left.

"Did you give him a ticket?" Jan asked as soon as both officers were back.

"Actually, the validation sticker had fallen off his plate. The Corporal gave him a blue slip, a checkup, which means the driver has ten days to get another licence-plate tag and show up at a detachment to prove it," Willow explained.

"Were you nervous?" Jan had felt anxious watching and couldn't imagine what it must be like to walk into an unknown situation many times a day.

Willow screwed her face up. "Not nervous, but cautious. And scrambling to remember everything I was taught about pulling over a car."

"You did fine," Sloan commented as he finished the paperwork. "I felt safer knowing you were checking my six. Covering my back," he explained for Jan. "And we have it all recorded for posterity." He patted the camera that was fixed to the dash.

The excitement over, they continued toward Bow Falls.

"Do you stop people for speeding a lot, Willow?" Jan had never thought about the routine work an officer performed every day on the job.

"Oh, I do a lot more than this, Jan. I also help out with the Teen Anti-Drug Program, with Gang Awareness, and with community policing, in addition to a lot of behind-the-scenes work that civilians — that's you," she winked at Jan, "don't realize goes on. I patrolled the back country on a quad last week. Screaming around on a four-wheeled all-terrain vehicle was a blast."

Jan sat back in her seat. She was amazed at how

much was involved in Willow's job. "I thought you stayed in the office and did computer input."

"Sounds soft, but no such luck." Willow turned back to Corporal Sloan. "About the poaching — do you know if it's one person or more?"

The two members picked up their previous conversation as though the incident with the Subaru was nothing. Jan realized that, to them, it *was* nothing, simply routine.

"We're working on the assumption it's one person. A small but effective operation." Sloan waited for the light to change, then started across the old stone bridge that crossed the Bow River, upstream of the famous falls.

"Any evidence left at the scene, like shell casings, tire tracks, or footprints?" Willow's voice seemed the tiniest bit stressed to Jan, which was a surprise. Willow had been so cool when they'd stopped the car.

The big officer sucked air between his teeth. "This guy's smooth. Nothing at the scene except dead bears."

They drove down the tightly winding road that ended at Bow Falls. Willow had said she'd never been to this picturesque spot, but instead of admiring the tumbling water and commenting on the beauty of the foam-flecked cascade as other first-timers did, she watched Sloan, her eyes never leaving his face. "Have you looked anywhere else for similar poaching cases?"

"I thought you wanted to see the Falls. Stop

yapping and have a look," the older officer instructed gruffly.

Willow tore her eyes away from Sloan and admired Mother Nature's beautiful handiwork. "I guess hordes of tourists appreciate the fact that Grandfather Falls situated himself a stone's throw from the centre of town." She pointed at a gaggle of Japanese tourists busily snapping pictures of each other with the falls in the background.

They continued on their patrol and, as Jan listened, she was astonished at how much Willow knew about grizzlies, hunting techniques, and the most effective ways to attract a bear. Several points she mentioned would work nicely on Jan's web site, like the fact that in the fall bears consumed 35,000 calories a day as they fattened up for their long winter hibernation. This explained why they were so hungry and so dangerous in that season.

"What happens to the parts once they're …" Jan looked for the right word, "harvested?"

Sloan hit his hand on the steering wheel. "Black market, that's what! The amount of money a gall bladder goes for would set you on your rump."

"The biggest market is in Asia," Willow added. "Bear parts are used in Chinese herbal medicines. Huge bucks and no questions asked. There are synthetics available, but apparently there's no substitute for the real thing."

When they stopped at the imposing Banff Springs Hotel in response to a call, Willow stayed with Jan while Sloan went in. Jan looked at the meticulously groomed gardens leading up to towering stone walls accented by balconies with ornate stone balustrades. The whole place had the feel of a fairy-tale castle. It was spectacular!

"Wow! How come we never came here on one of your mini-tours?" Willow asked, her head hanging out the window as she looked up at the imposing structure.

"I didn't think you'd be interested in an old hotel," Jan answered honestly.

"This isn't any old hotel, Jan. This is like something out of Disneyland!" Willow whistled as she continued to gawk.

"Willow," Jan said hesitantly, "you and Corporal Sloan have been talking about hunting. But I thought Native people didn't believe in killing bears, you know, that all life is sacred."

"Jan, a lot of people are mixed up about our beliefs. To First Nations people the grizzly bear is a powerful ally. We can ask for his help and protection, and yes, at times his life, if it is to sustain our own. We hunt bears, but we respect the sacrifice the animal is making and are thankful to the Creator for sending it to us when we need food. We appreciate the way all life works together, some giving so others can live." Her voice became sad. "It's when we kill for the wrong reasons or waste the animal's meat, like the poacher does, that problems happen. Remember when I said whatever energy you put out, good or bad, is what you will attract? If someone becomes corrupt, they put out the welcome mat for evil."

"And bring bad things like *wittigos*?" Jan asked.

Willow looked around as though expecting to see a wraith swoop down the grey walls of the old stone hotel. "They come like flies to rotting meat."

Jan shivered.

Corporal Sloan returned and continued the previous conversation. "S.S. Whitecloud, you know a lot about hunting grizzly, almost as much as me!" He barked a laugh. "What's your favourite bait?"

Willow scrunched up her face. "I'd have to say an old standard, Ten Dead Horses, is still my pick to click."

Sloan mulled this over for a moment. "Rankest smelling concoction out there, and one any bear within ten miles will come to check out. Good choice."

"What's Ten Dead Horses smell like?" Jan asked.

Both Willow and Sloan turned to look at her and started to laugh uproariously.

Jan realized it had been a dumb question. "Right — Ten Dead Horses! The name kind of gives it away. Gross!"

"I suppose you two want lunch now?" The corporal's tone was surly and Jan wondered if she'd overstayed her welcome.

"I think we deserve some grub." Willow checked her watch. "We missed coffee break and I have to check something out after work, so I won't have time to eat."

"What do you want?" he asked tersely.

Willow thought a moment. "There must be some local squat-and-gobble that has burgers and fries."

Sloan grumbled, but drove them to a hamburger joint. "You order, I'll pay," he instructed.

A smile broke across Willow's face. "In that case, we should have gone someplace for steak and lobster!"

Sloan snorted. "Don't push your luck, Rookie."

Willow's nerve at joking with Sloan made Jan realize how close two officers could become in a short space of time. When you relied on someone to perhaps prevent you from being killed, it would be natural for a bond to form very quickly. She wondered about the conversation she'd heard. Jan now knew the most amazing things about poaching bears and what to do with the parts afterward.

Chapter 10

When Jan returned home from the ride-along, some of the things Willow had said kept replaying in her head. Willow's specialized knowledge of bear hunting was amazing. Even Corporal Sloan had been impressed. Jan remembered seeing Willow in Wapiti Trail Outfitters right after they'd found out Dyer's gun may have been the one used in the poaching. And what about the time Willow had been so broke they'd climbed Sulphur Mountain instead of taking the gondola, when a week later she'd paid for an expensive lunch? But the incident that really set the bells clanging was catching Willow in David's study. She was sure Willow was lying.

Individually, none of these things was terribly suspicious, but put them together and it made a different picture, one Jan didn't like at all.

Several other bothersome details skittered around in Jan's brain, but she couldn't get a fix on them. She needed to find a logical answer for all these crazy incidents. Maybe a quick look in Willow's room might shed more light on things. If Jan could find a letter or list or, better yet, a tell-all diary to explain what was going on, she was sure everything would be explained. What would it hurt? Willow was still at work and Jan was only going to have a peek around.

The room looked the same. The dresser was still covered with the coloured cloths and strange artifacts. The bowl in the middle of the dresser had ash residue that Jan assumed was from Willow's latest sweetgrass smudging. She looked in the closet and felt foolish as she checked under the bed. Nothing.

As she turned to leave, the laptop caught her eye. She'd already snooped in real space; it seemed only reasonable she take a tour of Willow's e-space. Jan booted up the computer.

She tried to open the folders, but most of them were password protected. There was one labelled *maps*. Jan remembered Willow's map with all the dots marking must-see hot spots. She wondered what new tourist attractions Willow had added to her itinerary and clicked on the folder.

Surprisingly, there were two map files listed, one for Banff National Park and one for the Rainbow Lake Area. Jan opened the one for Banff. More dots of different colours were scattered across the map at odd locations. There was even a red dot near the gate at the east boundary of the park. Jan wondered, *Why there?* She checked the other points, frowning at the unlikely places Willow had visited.

As Jan studied the locations of the markers more closely, something about the map began to look eerily familiar. Suddenly, she remembered the poaching map on the government database. Hurrying to her own room, Jan retrieved the printouts from Liam's spectacular hack, checked the names of the sites where the bears had been killed, and compared the information with that on Willow's computer. Both had exactly the same spots marked!

The points corresponded precisely, except for the one at the east boundary. Jan remembered David telling her there'd been a poaching near the east gate. That piece of data hadn't been on the Fish and Wildlife site when she and Liam had hacked in. Was it there now? Was Willow using information from that site to fill in the points on her map?

Jan went to her room and fired up her computer. Opening the Internet connections, she went to Liam's favourite computer geek chat room and looked for his nickname — WizardOne. As she suspected, he was online, along with twenty-two other bit heads. Jan signed in, using her name of WickedWheels. "W1, hey, it's me," she typed.

"Hi, WW! This isn't your usual hangout. What's up?" The reply from Liam flashed onto the screen.

"Let's P2P," Jan typed, instructing Liam to meet her in a private chat room so they could talk without the whole universe eavesdropping.

"Poof, I'm gone!"

Once in the messaging room, Jan typed in her request. "Wiz, can you do me a favour and get back into that Special Site?" She hoped he'd figure out what she meant. Even though they were supposed to be in a private room with no prying eyes, she didn't want to chance naming the restricted Alberta Fish and Wildlife government site they'd hacked into.

"I love it when a woman asks me to colour outside the lines. (LOL) Why?"

She knew Liam understood. Jan wasn't sure how to ask him what she needed. "Can you get info on any tragic deaths near the east gate?"

Liam was nothing if not quick on the uptake. "No problem. Give me ten and I'll e-mail you. I'm bailing now."

Jan got out of the chat room, opened her e-mail program, and waited.

Eight minutes later, she heard the familiar bell and the message *You've got mail!* popped up. She opened Liam's e-mail.

"Nothing listed or mentioned. What's this about?"

Jan wasn't ready to talk to Liam yet. She had to make sense of this first. She hit Reply and typed, "Thanks, Wiz. I'll explain later. :)"

Jan wondered how Willow had known to mark

that site. She said she hadn't talked to David in days, but it was possible he'd told her and she'd forgotten to mention it. Remembering she hadn't shut down Willow's computer, Jan hustled back to the other bedroom. Before closing the map file, she searched the screen for the red dot she'd seen the morning after Willow had arrived — Iron Rock Canyon, the site of the very first poaching.

The dots must all be markers for poaching sites. Why was Willow keeping track of the killings? Was it part of her data-entry job with Fish and Wildlife, or was she simply curious? Jan thought of the summer student's avid interest in every-thing to do with the grizzlies, especially the poaching and the spring hunt.

She closed the Banff map file and was about to shut the computer down when she again noticed the file marked *Rainbow Lake Area*. Curious, Jan opened it, then stared at the screen. This map had a similar shotgun blast of dots.

Trusting a hunch, Jan ran for her phone. When it came to speed, sometimes the old-fashioned methods were the best. E-mailing took a while and right now she needed every minute. "Liam, you have to come over *now*."

"Can't I help you over the computer again? I'm in the middle of something."

Jan knew the something was probably a high-stakes computer game with his cyber-buddies. She shifted tactics. "I need your unique talents."

There was a heavy sigh at the other end of the

phone line, but Jan knew her bait would work. If there was a chance of a hack, Liam was in. "Okay. I'll be there in fifteen." He hung up without saying goodbye.

Exactly fifteen minutes later, Liam was at her door. "What's up, Buttercup?"

"Come and have a look at this." She took him to Willow's room and showed him the map of Rainbow Lake on the computer. "Can you get back into the government site and see if there were grizzlies poached near those spots?'

A sly grin lit Liam's face. "You're really getting into this hacking stuff! I can't believe it. You're the one who was worried about the G-men tracking us down."

"Never mind the I-told-you-so's." She motioned to the door. "I don't want Willow to know we were on her computer, so you'll have to use mine for the hack."

"This is too cool." Liam went to Jan's room and she heard him accessing the Net. After several minutes and the sound of a lot of keyboarding, he called out, "Your wish is my command!"

"Right on," Jan yelled back. "Tell me if these names are there." She read out the names of the sites marked by the dots on Willow's computer map. Liam answered yes to every one. They were all illegal grizzly kills.

"Jan, the thing is, it looks like the data on that map is from the spring of last year," Liam added.

Jan filed this away under O for Odd. There had

to be a logical and innocent explanation for everything. She refused to believe what popped into her head — the obvious thought, the truly tough thought, the unbelievable unthinkable terrible thought that Willow Whitecloud was the Banff Grizzly Poacher. Had she cleaned out the bears at Rainbow Lake last year and was now doing the same here? Jan sat down heavily on the bed.

No way. It couldn't be true. But the list of suspicious occurrences against Willow was getting longer by the minute. Jan had to get to the bottom of this.

"Why'd you want this info?" Liam asked as he walked back into Willow's room.

Jan decided a fresh, more rational perspective was exactly what she needed. "Every one of those points is a grizzly kill site. For some reason, Willow is keeping track of poached bears."

Liam's sunglasses slipped down his forehead and he pushed them back into his tawny hair. "No kidding. For how long?"

"At least since last year back in Rainbow Lake, and it looks like from the minute she arrived here. I remember seeing the red marker for the Iron Rock Canyon kill on her computer the morning after she arrived!"

Liam frowned. "Whoa, the *next* morning? I never heard about the poaching until you told me. It wasn't on the Net anywhere."

"And I found out about it when Corporal Sloan came to tell David at breakfast Friday morning.

116

Trust me, it was news to David too. Liam, that means she'd marked the sight *before* Corporal Sloan told us!" Jan felt sick.

"That means she knew earlier that morning or even the night before," Liam said.

"And the kill at the east park gate — she had that one marked before it was posted on the Fish and Wildlife site. Maybe David told her. I've got to find out." She yanked her cell phone out of her jeans pocket and dialled David's number.

"Hi, it's me. Hey, I'm working on my bears of Banff computer project for school and was wondering — when did the poaching at the east gate go public?"

"And a polite hello to you to, January. I guess that bit of news was released to the media two days after we became involved. It was pretty well on a need-to-know basis before that."

"Right. So the only ones who knew would be other RCMP officers, like Corporal Sloan and Willow."

David hesitated. "Actually, I was waiting to give Corporal Sloan a full written report, and I didn't discuss it with Willow at all. There was no reason. What's with all the questions?" David used that tone adults get when they know kids are up to something.

Jan didn't want to get into it. "Just updating my bear web site. See you tonight." She hung up before David could ask her anything else. She turned to Liam. "Willow knew before God did."

She thought of something else, something more ominous. "The day before the first poaching at Iron Rock," she squinted her eyes trying to get it straight, "that would be Thursday, there was a rifle reported stolen from the same area. What if Willow stole that gun? Liam," her voice trembled slightly. "What if she's the Banff Poacher?"

"Let's not jump to any rash conclusions. Willow didn't get here until Friday, remember? You took off from school that afternoon like a bat out of hell," Liam reminded her.

"Right, Willow said the drive from Edmonton had been a long, tough one. Her bike was dirty and I remember seeing red mud caked on the tires. How does it all tie together? Think, Fournier, think." Jan stared at the ancient wooden plank floor as she tried to make sense of it all. She tried to see the answer in the soft gleam of the old-fashioned paste wax.

"Hey, remember we talked about Iron Rock Canyon and I told you the dirt there was bright red," Liam raised his eyebrows.

Jan's head came up instantly as she made the same connection. "Like the mud on Willow's tires." Something stirred at the back of her mind, something she'd overlooked. With a jolt, she remembered. "Liam, Willow had lots of time to steal the rifle. She was here *two days* before coming to our house."

"How do you know that?" he asked.

"I found a park pass in her backpack and it was

dated for the Wednesday before she arrived." Jan's mind whirled. "There are a lot of strange things going on here." She looked at the computer again, remembering the *Bear Licences — Drawn Names* and *Bear Licenses — Substituted Names* files she'd seen. "Since you're doing such a fabulous job of altered access, do you think you could bust a password on a couple of protected files?"

Liam rubbed his hands together and his lips curved into a wicked smile. "What do you think?"

Jan couldn't help but notice the way his incredibly blue eyes glimmered invitingly when he looked at her, and she suddenly hoped it wasn't entirely because of the prospect of more hacking.

Willow had several security measures in place to keep snoopy people from inadvertently seeing what she had stored, and Liam took this as a direct challenge. "The two files you want are *Drawn Names* and *Substituted Names?*" he asked, deftly sliding through Willow's hard drive like a ghost.

"To start," Jan said, moving closer to read the screen over Liam's shoulder. She noticed that, for a guy, he smelled terrific. "We might need to check out other stuff too." Her eyes skimmed the *Drawn Names* file. "Am I crazy, or does this look like an official Alberta Fish and Wildlife file?" She finished reading the information on those hunters who had been lucky enough to have their WINs come up for the spring hunt. "How about the *Substituted Names?*"

Liam opened the file. "You're right. These have

been hacked from an encrypted site. Willow must be a kick-ass code slinger to have gotten in."

Jan knew this had become a serious game. Willow was not what she seemed to be. "Yeah, but working for the RCMP must help. She'd have clearance for some restricted sites, right?"

"And …" Rubbing his chin, Liam seemed to be mulling something over. He paused so long, Jan punched him on the shoulder. "What, for crying out loud!"

"Didn't you tell me she volunteered to do some data inputting for Fish and Wildlife? I don't think she did that to be a helpful Girl Scout. It would give her access to the *IP*s of other Fish and Wildlife employees — ones with higher security clearances. She could use one of them to get past a lot of the firewalls without alerting the intrusion-detection systems, and the signature left would look legit."

Jan didn't understand most of what Liam said, but figured this was how Willow had accessed the data she had. "Look at that!" Jan exclaimed as she read the screen. "It shows the names from the *Drawn* file have been changed to the ones listed in the *Substituted* file." She checked the addresses. "Hey, most of these permits are mailed to box numbers in Calgary and Airdrie, not to street addresses."

"You know …" Liam dragged out his sentence and Jan shot him a warning glance. He took the hint and quickly went on. "If I wanted to corner the market on bear licences, I'd break into the Government of Alberta Fish and Wildlife database and replace legitimate winners with fake ones, so that licences would go to postal boxes I'd set up, and I'd be the only one out there hunting the bears."

With a sinking feeling in her stomach, Jan understood where Liam was going. "And if I was a poacher," she continued the line of thought, "I sure wouldn't want any other hunters bagging my bears, since there aren't that many around. You know, from a hunter's point of view it makes perfect sense."

She and Liam looked at each other. It appeared they'd found their poacher, and her name was Willow Whitecloud.

Jan shook her head so hard she felt dizzy. "Willow is not the poacher, Liam! There has to be another explanation! She's always going on about the forces of good and evil. This would put her on the board of directors of Evil Incorporated. These files must mean something else."

Liam gave her a skeptical look. "Yeah? What? You said yourself that Willow had marked all the kill sites before anyone knew they were kill sites. Remember the red mud on her tires? She had last year's northern kills on a map, and I seem to remember you telling me that Willow's an authority on how to profitably dispose of bear parts! Jan, you do the dot-to-dot. We have to tell David *now*." He reached for his cell phone.

"No." Jan snatched the phone out of Liam's

hand. "This could all be circumstantial. If we report it, we'll put Willow in front of a firing squad. We both know she hacked into those restricted sites. If even just that comes out, her chances of a career with the RCMP will be finished. She could go to jail!"

"I know she's your friend but, January, if she's the poacher, we could be putting the few remaining bears at risk. Do you want to gamble the life of a grizzly? The bears belong to all of us, and I don't want one more of *my* bears ending up in some opium den in China!" He held his hand out for his phone.

Jan clutched the phone to her chest. She knew it wasn't Willow but, man, it looked bad. "I'll make you a deal. Let me go find Willow. I'll bring her back here and we can confront her together. She can explain how she's actually working undercover for CSIS to get the bad guys and we'll all kick back and have a good laugh." Liam hesitated. "We owe her that."

Jan walked over to the bear fetish with the spectacular necklace and touched one of the shiny claws. "She's not the poacher, Liam." Jan turned to look at him. "Willow told me that what you put out into the world sticks with you. She said we go on forever, and I know she wouldn't want to spend eternity as a creepy *wittigo*. We have to find out the truth."

Sighing, Liam came and put his arms around her. "Jan, what if we already have?"

His voice was kind and tinged with a whisper of regret. Jan knew he didn't want it to be Willow either. She rested her head on Liam's shoulder. It was strange confiding in a guy, but Liam wasn't really *a guy* — he was, well, he was Liam! Her eye fell on a printout beside the computer. She sprang away from Liam like she'd been burned.

"Look at this!" She snatched up the paper. It was a map of The Three Widows Golf Resort development, located a short distance from the park boundary. "Willow said she had to check out something after work. I bet it was at The Three Widows." She gave him a quick hug. "You wait here while I go get her. Play computer games, hack into the FBI, or buy something on eBay, just don't go to David with any of this, not yet. I'm sure Willow will be able to clear everything up in five minutes."

Liam gave her a skeptical look. "And if she can't?"

"If she can't, we all go to David." Jan ran out of the room and down the stairs to her bike.

Chapter 11

The ride was wild. Jan had her throttle cranked open as she danced through the corners and rocketed down the straights. She flew past slower-moving cars on the highway, so focused she hardly noticed them.

Jan heard that construction at The Three Widows Golf Resort had been halted because of a bear problem. The bruins had discovered the tasty garbage left behind by careless crews and had taken full advantage of the windfall. Unfortunately, this made working in the area hazardous, and the developer had demanded that Fish and Wildlife do something to get rid of the bears. Inside the park, it would be the responsibility of the park wardens; because it was outside Banff National Park, Alberta Fish and Wildlife had handled the problem.

As Jan stashed her bike at the bottom of a steep path that led to the construction site, the afternoon sun slid behind one of the three peaks that gave the resort its name. The area was immediately plunged into gloom.

Using all the teen-stealth techniques she'd mastered from sneaking in late at night, Jan began climbing. Through the pines up ahead Jan spotted Willow's bike. What could Willow be doing at a closed work site like this?

Scanning the construction site, she saw Willow. She didn't know whether to be relieved or worried. What if whatever Willow was doing here somehow confirmed Liam's accusation?

Jan tried to move like a shadow as she drew closer to her quarry. She stepped on a dry branch and the snapping noise made her cringe. It seemed incredibly loud in the stillness. Apparently, her ancestral hunting skills were sadly lacking. Jan checked to see if Willow had heard the racket, but the tall girl seemed oblivious.

Jan inched closer as she dodged from tree to tree and hid behind bushes. She could see why Willow had come. Placed around the edges of the work site were three large metal containers mounted on wheels. They looked like giant barrels laid on their sides with one end open. Jan knew that inside the barrels would be pieces of rotting meat. They were bear traps!

Fish and Wildlife was trying to catch the bears. Jan hoped it was to transport them out of the area and not to destroy them. As she watched, Willow went to each trap and sprung the door closed.

The noise of the metal clanging shut echoed in

the high mountain meadow. When Willow had finished, she turned and looked directly at where Jan was hiding. "You can come out now, January." The authority in her voice was hard to resist.

Jan didn't know what to do. Was Willow bluffing or did she know that Jan was here? Looking around, Jan judged the distance to her bike in case she needed to get out of there in a hurry. The problem was that Willow was bigger than Jan, and extremely fit. Willow had acted like the hike up Sulphur Mountain was a stroll in the park. She could probably outrun Jan and not break a sweat.

Jan stepped out from behind the tall pine. "Uh … hi! How's it going?"

Willow looked at her icily. "Cut the small talk, Jan. Why are you following me?"

Jan tried to think of the best way to tell Willow they had to go back to the house so she and Liam could confront her about being a nasty, low-life poacher. Nothing brilliant came to mind. Maybe she should lie, but that didn't seem right. Besides, if Willow were the bad guy, she and her *wittigo* posse would be able to spot the lie in a heartbeat. The truth seemed best, at least partial truth. "I need you to come home with me right now."

"Why? Is something wrong?"

Jan could hear the suspicion in Willow's voice. "Actually yes, and Liam and I need to talk to you about it. We're worried." This was totally true.

Willow gave her a skeptical look and Jan tried to regroup, marvelling at her own talent for making even the truth sound like a lie. She tried the indirect approach. "Since you're done with the traps, we can go." It occurred to her that she was missing an obvious question, which might prove important. "So, why are you springing them anyway?"

Willow drew herself up to her full height, which was impressive. "That's none of your business." She stalked over to her bike.

Jan saw the fury in the girl's eyes and, although her heart had climbed into her throat, she tried to act cool. "There's no reason to be such a be-yotch! I was just wondering, that's all."

Willow turned to confront her. "Fine! It's simple. The bears belong here. They wouldn't be a threat if some rich bastard hadn't decided the world needed another golf course. If the developer would stop building for a couple of weeks, the bears would move on, and there would be no need to trap and transport them hundreds of kilometres away from their home range." She climbed on her bike and hit the starter. "Consider this your only warning. Stay out of my business."

"Willow, wait! I'm serious. You have to come back home with me." Jan ran and grabbed her arm. Even through the leather riding jacket she could feel the muscles.

Willow stared down at Jan's hand. "It's dangerous to poke around in someone else's business. For your own health, stay out of mine!"

Jan looked at the traps. She didn't like the idea

of shuffling the bears away so the golf course could be built anymore than Willow did. But if Willow was the poacher, stopping the bears from being moved would also increase her chances of another kill.

No matter what the consequences, the bear killing had to stop or the grizzlies of Banff would end up as close to extinction as the pandas in China, the tigers in India, or the codfish in Newfoundland.

Jan took a deep breath, trying to slow the jackhammer pounding of her heart. If Willow was the poacher, she had to be stopped *now*. "I know why you don't want the bears relocated, and it has nothing to do with you having their well-being in mind."

Willow's face was a study in confusion. "What are you talking about?"

"I know all about the poaching and changing the names of the hunters drawn for a grizzly licence."

Willow's tone cut like a chainsaw. "How do you know any of that?"

"Never mind how. I know you were in the park two days before you showed up at our house, which put you here when the rifle was stolen from Dyer. It would also give you time to kill that bear at Iron Rock Canyon. Did you know that when the iron leaches out of the rocks, it oxidizes and turns the dirt bright red? Your tires were covered in red mud when you first arrived at our house. You're almost a cop, figure it out. What do you think your fellow officers are going to think when they hear all this? Willow, you look like the perfect candidate for the poacher."

Willow killed the engine and climbed off her bike.

Jan had her full attention now. "Even Corporal Sloan was amazed at how much you knew about hunting bears. What better place to bag bears than in a national park where you would be the only hunter? You said you'd recently come into some cash. Making a big score on gall bladders and paws would explain how you could be completely broke one week and afford to take Liam and me out to a fancy restaurant the next."

Willow looked like Jan had run over her with a steamroller. For a moment she was speechless, then she shook her head. "You've got this all wrong." She took a menacing step toward Jan.

Chapter 12

Jan felt her hands ball into fists and she tried to recall everything she had learned in the self-defence course she'd taken. She should wait until Willow lunged for her, then use the girl's own momentum to throw her to the ground. That was it. She flexed her knees, lowering her centre of gravity.

Willow stopped. "I didn't kill those bears, Jan. That money was my first paycheque. I spent it on you two because you're my friends. Didn't you notice I was back to peanut butter sandwiches after that lunch? I was broke again and barely had enough to put gas in my tank. That cash I came into was money my grandfather left me when he died. I blew it all to pay off my bike."

"I want to be on your team, Willow, but it looks bad, even to me." Despite Willow's explanations, there were still a lot of big holes. As everything flooded through Jan's mind, she felt her faith in

Willow's innocence start to waver under the weight of all she and Liam had discovered. "I need you to prove to me you didn't do this terrible thing. I think you're about the coolest person I know. You and your smudging and sweat lodges. You made me think about things, weird things like spirit helpers and talking to dead people. I don't want it all to have been some smokescreen to divert me from getting too close to the truth. I want to believe." She felt the edges of her eyes prickle with tears.

Willow folded her arms and calmly waited for Jan to finish, then she raised an eyebrow. The gesture reminded Jan uncomfortably of the way Liam looked right before he hit her with something really outrageous.

"Are you through, Miss Thinks-She's-Got-It-Figured-Out-But-Who-Actually-Has-It-All-Backwards?"

Jan blinked at her. "What?" She'd poured out her soul and this was what she got?

"You dope. You've got all the puzzle pieces, but it's like you don't have the box lid to see what the real picture looks like. You've put the pieces together wrong. I didn't kill those bears, Todd Dyer did." Willow waited while Jan processed the words.

Todd Dyer, the guide? Jan's mind flashed to the computer map of Alberta with all the poaching at Rainbow Lake the previous year. Willow was from Rainbow Lake, and the bears didn't start dying in Banff until Willow showed up here. With a start Jan realized what else Willow had said. "Hey, who are you calling a dope?"

Willow laughed. "Jeez," she looked around. "You seem to be the only one here who fits that description." Her tone became serious. "Come on, let's get away from this trap. The smell of that rank meat is turning my stomach."

She led Jan over to a makeshift bench of a plank laid across two stumps. "I think you know enough of this puzzle to be dangerous — to me! This is how it all really happened. Last year, we had a bear poached in Rainbow Lake. It was a grizzly, but not just any grizzly. It was one our band had raised from a cub. Actually, my grandfather had taken it upon himself to save the little guy. He fed that cub, taught it how to catch fish in the stream, showed it where to find the best grubs under logs — all the things a mother bear would have taught the cub if she'd been around. But she'd been poached and the cub, hiding in the den, was left to die. For twenty years, my grandfather and that bear were best friends."

Jan heard a tiny quaver in Willow's voice and realized how hard it was for her to talk about this piece of her family history.

"My grandfather found the bear as it was dying, slashed to pieces by Todd Dyer. Only he called himself Fred Todd then. Nimosôm was never the same again. Dyer didn't kill only the bear; part of my grandfather died that night. As the months

132

wore on, he became frailer and frailer until he was a shadow walking. I knew Dyer was a guide in Rainbow Lake, and thought it was suspicious that the poaching started when he showed up. When I heard that Dyer left the area in a big hurry, I decided to check him out by using a little creative hacking. That's how I knew he was coming here to Banff."

Jan listened, saddened for Willow, but she was relieved that her faith hadn't been misplaced. It was a lot to take in. The wind sighed in the trees as a squirrel darted directly behind her. Startled by the swift movement, Jan jumped, nearly slipping off the bench. "Okay, I believe you. How did you end up here working for the RCMP?"

"All I had was my grandfather, and he was fading from this world, living more and more with the spirits. I had to get Dyer for what he did to that bear and my grandfather. When one of the RCMP officers at Rainbow told me about the Summer Student Program, and that he could pull some strings and get me posted to Banff, I knew it was my chance to get that creep. My grandfather wanted me to put the hatred out of my heart, to stay on the reserve and be a shaman for my people, but I couldn't let Dyer get away with it. We argued, but I left anyway. While I was away at the RCMP training, he died. I never got a chance to say I was sorry for quarrelling with him, or to thank him for raising me to follow the Sweetgrass Trail. His spirit rides the wind now. He won't find peace until I do, and that means stopping Dyer. Jan, you could help me."

Jan sat in silence trying to comprehend everything. Then the questions began. "What about the stolen rifle? Why were you here in Banff early? How did you know to go to Iron Rock Canyon the day the grizzly was poached?"

Willow held up her hand to try to stop the avalanche. "Whoa! There's one thing I haven't told you." She took a deep breath. "I think Dyer had serious help to pull this off. He was e-mailing someone, someone who helped set the whole thing up."

Jan was rocked. "Dyer was e-mailing another poacher?"

Willow went on. "I was able to tap into Dyer's e-mails. Two days before I was scheduled to leave for Banff, Dyer sent one that said he was going to "bag a bear tonight in Iron Rock" because his Chinese client needed the paws. I rode like Death was chasing me and made it from Edmonton in a touch under three-and-a-half hours, but by that time it was dark and I had trouble finding the right canyon. I was too late." Absently, she rubbed at a spot of grease on her jeans as though it was a sin she had to shed. "I think Dyer reported his gun stolen so he'd be in the clear if the casings or registration were traced back to him. I went to the store and tried to buy shells for a rifle of the same make. He said the store didn't stock them, but he could sell me a box from his own supply. He said he needed the rest for himself. This was supposed to be *after* the gun was stolen. I've spent my nights tracking down clues trying to anticipate where the jerk would strike next. Didn't you wonder about me when I was out every night clubbing?"

"I thought you were just incredibly sociable and maybe looking for a man." Jan felt a little foolish admitting this. "I knew you were innocent. Liam wanted to go to David, but I've convinced him to wait till you have a chance to explain. I think he'll be glad you're not the poacher too."

Willow's face hardened. "Jan, we can't tell David anything about this. He'll file a report in the computer and Dyer will run again. Dyer must have access to the RCMP database to get the files he uses. But I've seen him with electronics. He can't even operate the digital cash terminal in the store! He must have someone else helping him …"

Jan stared at her. "A partner who has access to the RCMP database!"

Jan thought of Liam waiting to call David. "Come on. We've going to talk to Liam. You can tell him your story and then we'll let him do some creative hacking of his own."

* * *

Jan and Willow rode home at warp speed. Willow could tell Liam the path to break into Dyer's e-mail, and then Liam could tell if it was a fake.

When they arrived, the girls quickly filled Liam in.

"Dyer's the villain in this, and he's not alone." Jan had already decided a preemptive strike was the best way to make Liam listen. "Willow's going to tell you how she got into his e-mail, then we'll have a look for ourselves to make sure this is the real deal." She gave Liam a hard stare that said that this was the proof he needed, to just shut up and hack. Liam was up to speed in a nanosecond, and Jan had the odd sensation that she and Liam were on exactly the same wavelength, that words were hardly necessary.

"I feel I should warn you, Willow," Liam said in a no-nonsense tone that made Jan give him an *oh brother* look. "As one hacker to another, I can spot a hoax a mile away. If this is bogus, I'll drive Jan to the RCMP myself so she can turn you in."

"I'm not the poacher!" Willow waved her arms in exasperation. "Okay, you want proof? Let's go, Hotshot." She recited a complicated set of keystrokes that Liam executed in a heartbeat.

"How'd you figure out his password?" Liam asked as he continued typing.

"Mr. Dyer isn't very imaginative. He used *Grizzly*, a real no-brainer to crack." Willow gave a half-hearted laugh.

Liam scanned the screen, then wiggled his eyebrows at Jan. "Have a look. These are the real deal."

Jan read the list of e-mails. "Which one talked about the kill in Iron Rock?" she asked Willow.

136

Willow pointed to the screen. "That one. And you might like to see those, too." She pointed to two more. "They talk about shipping bear parts to his overseas contact."

Jan and Liam read the messages.

"Okay." Jan knew what they had to do. "We should work together to figure out who his partner is. Three heads have got to be better than one."

Willow's face broke into a wide grin. "And pooling our information would close this case in a big hurry."

Liam tapped the screen with his pen, which had a model of the starship Enterprise stuck on to the end. "Why can't we go to the RCMP with these e-mails? They prove Dyer is the bad guy."

Willow's eyes were like thunderclouds. "Simple. We can't go because Dyer's partner may be an RCMP officer."

Liam and Jan stared back mutely as the full meaning of her statement hit them. A thought struck Jan, one she didn't like at all. "That's why you were snooping in David's study. You were checking to see if he was in on this!"

Willow looked at her sheepishly. "Yeah, I was. But look at it from my point of view — David would be a logical suspect. The poaching started after he was posted here, and he's the liaison with the park warden's office. If it walks like a duck and talks like a duck …"

"Stuff your ducks, Willow!" Jan exploded. "David is the good guy here."

"Take it easy, Jan. I know that now, but I had to make sure." Willow glared right back at Jan.

"I need to say something." Liam broke in, scattering the tension. "Willow, when I thought you were the poacher, it sucked. I should have known better and I'm sorry. Jan likes you a lot," he shot Jan a look and she quirked her mouth into a reluctant smile. She knew he was right. "And believe me, nothing's worse than finding out your hero has feet of clay."

"When a hero seems to slip, Liam, it's not because he has feet of clay, but because we refuse to let him be human." Willow's voice was so low it was almost a whisper.

Liam, however, reacted as though she'd shouted at him. "Yeah, well there's a reason we call them heroes. They're supposed to do the right thing."

Jan was amazed and a little shocked at his outburst. Hastily, she tried to get the meeting back on track. She didn't like to see Liam upset. "Hold on. The reason we're all here is that we need to stop Dyer and his partner. And to tell the authorities before any more bears die." Her gaze took in both Liam and Willow. She could see Liam refocus. He looked at her and cleared his throat. "You're right, Jan. The bears' immediate safety is our first priority."

Willow stood up. "Let's get everything in order first. Until we know who Dyer's partner is, we might be reporting this crime to one of the criminals."

Jan hesitated. She didn't want David to worry

about this case one second longer than he had to.

"I know, Jan. I want this to end too." It was as though Willow had read Jan's mind. "But we can't go to David accusing an RCMP officer until we know all the details."

She left and Jan felt her knees go wobbly. Liam pushed a stool toward her. "Uh, if you want me to hang around, we can finish the last details on our project. You have the race tomorrow, and the project is due Monday."

He looked at her with his bluer-than-blue eyes shining and a lanky blond curl falling over his forehead. Jan had to smile. "Good thinking, Wiz. With the race and the poaching, our poor web site has kind of been pushed to the back burner." She took the seat he'd offered. Spending what was left of her Saturday afternoon with B. Liam Simpson appealed to Jan — a lot.

They discussed the final finicky bits until Jan was sure their project would be firmly in the *A* category with Mr. Volk. Jan said she could finish her polishing later and offered Liam a soda before he left. Eventually, their conversation worked its way to Liam's dad. Liam said he still thought his dad was a first-class jerk for skipping out on him and his mom.

"Did he tell you to get lost?" Jan asked.

Liam's face went dark. "He didn't have to. He's running out on us, isn't he?"

Jan moved to the window seat of the dormer in her room. She looked out the window and saw a fat brown squirrel sitting on the outside sill. It was chewing apart a pine cone to get at the seeds. As she watched the chubby rodent, it stopped and looked at her with bright black eyes. The poor animal had a ragged ear, as if he'd had a close encounter of the ugly kind with something bigger and meaner.

Glancing at Liam, Jan knew he wasn't going to like what she had to say next. But it needed to be said. "I thought you told me your parents have been divorced for five years. Don't you think after five years they have the right to go on with their lives?" She hugged a pillow to her chest. "And didn't I see your mom come to church with Mr. Volk last week?" She gave Liam an inquiring look, but knew he couldn't deny it. "Don't we all deserve a chance at happiness without letting the past get in the way? If we keep looking behind us, how can we go forward?"

To her shock, Liam did an unprecedented thing. He shut off the computer and came to sit beside Jan.

"What are you saying? That I should accept being cut out of my dad's life?" His voice sounded a little choked.

"I remember when my dad died, I thought life would never be the same. And you know what? It wasn't, but that didn't mean it sucked. Life was different. My mom met David and they got married, Grey got his own place and opened a business, and we moved here, which was huge."

She tossed the pillow down and put her hand on Liam's arm. "A lot of things changed, but the end of the world never came. In fact, my life is pretty good right now. I know that change always happens and we'd better be able to adapt. Maybe if you swam with the current instead of fighting against it, you'd get to the other shore faster."

Liam's eyes glinted with what she decided would have been called tears if Liam were a girl — but guys didn't get all misty, did they? They sat together in companionable silence for a long time and watched the fat squirrel hiding pine cones under the trees.

* * *

After Liam left, Jan felt their friendship had gone to another level. She'd never talked to a guy like she'd talked to Liam. It had been a strange, but nice, experience.

Jan set to work finessing the last details of the project. An hour later, she'd completed all the adjustments and was about to add the part about contacting the park wardens for additional information when a pop-up flashed onto her screen.

"Oh, not now!" Jan moaned. The stupid ad would shut down her machine, and she hadn't saved her work. Before she could react, her screen lit up in a puff of brilliant orange smoke and a neon-green cartoon dragon appeared. It fluttered tiny, bright-pink wings and wore suspiciously familiar sunglasses. With a fiery blast, the fearsome dragon melted the pop-up until it dripped off the bottom of her screen. The friendly beast then wiggled its eyebrows and winked devilishly before disappearing in a puff of smoke.

Jan couldn't help herself. She began to giggle, then laugh until her sides hurt.

As she closed down her computer, her eye caught the time displayed in the corner of her screen. "Oh, no!" She flew downstairs to her bike. With everything that had happened that afternoon, she'd completely forgotten she was supposed to meet her mom at the church for Saturday night mass. If she didn't change clothes or worry about her hair, she could at least be there for the closing prayers.

There was no parking left in front of the old stone church when Jan arrived, so she had to find a spot down the street. As she ran into the church, she yanked off her helmet and jacket. She raked her fingers through her wild hair, which was damp with sweat and sticking out at weird angles. She glanced down at her jeans and cringed. They were her old worn favourites with both knees blown out. To finish off her vagrant vogue, she was wearing a too-tight T-shirt. Jan felt rotten. She'd not only shown up embarrassingly late, she looked like a refugee from a third-rate biker movie!

All hope of getting away with these minor indiscretions vanished when she saw that her mother was sitting in the middle of the front pew.

Trying to be as unobtrusive as possible, Jan eased her way into the back row. Father Simpson, who was in the middle of the blessing, spotted her and gave a quick nod as if to say, "better late than never." As she settled in her seat, Jan knew she'd have some explaining to do to her mom.

Jan had almost told her mom she wasn't going to go to mass, but with everything else happening she didn't want to cause her any more stress. The years when Jan had not gone to church had caused a lot of friction between her and her mom. Things had been much more peaceful since she'd started attending again. But was going to mass simply to keep peace in the house the thing to do?

Willow and her shamanism popped unbidden into Jan's head. The idea of nature and all life being intertwined and sacred was something Jan could get on board with. As was living your life the best you can and doing good for others, "following the Sweetgrass Trail" was what Willow had called it. It was the old golden rule — do unto others as you would have them do unto you.

After mass, Jan waited for her mom outside the church. She was prepared to apologize, but her mom just gave Jan's grubby outfit a critical glance and said "I'll see you at home, January," before heading for the car. Jan felt like she couldn't win.

When they got home, her mother stopped her before she could go up to her room. "We need to talk, Jan." Her mom's voice was gentle.

"Is this about me being late for mass? I'm

really sorry," Jan protested. "I was on the computer and lost track of time. And I was there for the end."

Jan's mom looked at her kindly, but her words were tinged with sadness. "It's not simply one mass, Jan. We both know that. This is more than a lapse of time; it's a lapse of a far greater kind. Maybe you should think this through, Honey. Perhaps you need to ask yourself what you truly believe is right for you."

Her mom kept a rosary in her purse and said prayers with them when she had a problem that required serious mulling. Even though they were nowhere in sight now, Jan saw her mother's fingers moving over the ghost beads.

Jan knew she couldn't avoid this conversation. "You're right, Mom. I've had a lot on my mind lately." It was hard to put her feelings into words. "I've been talking with Willow. There are lots of things about the old ways that I like. How there is a kind of sacredness to everything, and making right choices should be a lifestyle, not something we do in a crunch situation. She says we need to live the best way we can all the time." Jan shuddered involuntarily. "Willow also told me that if we're bad, we can attract evil to us."

As if she was caught in the sudden rush of an incoming tide, Jan felt completely out of her depth. "Mom, maybe I'm a bad person. Maybe I've always been bad."

Her mother's eyes searched Jan's, trying to

144

understand. "Honey, what are you talking about?"

"I mean, what if I really am a bad person deep down, and that's why I feel like I don't belong when I go to mass. Maybe God is telling me to leave his house." She couldn't stop talking. "Maybe God doesn't want me because of the accident, because of …" Her voice trailed off.

A look of comprehension flooded her mother's face. "Oh, January! Is this about your father's death?"

Jan swiped at the tears that overflowed and trickled down her cheeks. In a flash she was a little girl again, sitting in the back seat of their family car. The car began sliding out of control and her dad was yelling at her to hold on. They smashed violently into a huge tree. A brilliant red flower blossomed on the window where her dad's head hit. Crying, Jan promised to be a good girl forever and ever if he would just not leave her. But he did leave her, he died.

Jan thought of her dreams and the phantom figure she was unable to save. "Mom, if I'd been a better girl, maybe Daddy would have fought harder to stay, to live. Sometimes I get scared that if everything doesn't go right, David won't stay with us either. And it will be my fault, because deep down I'm a bad person and I attract bad energy."

Her mom pushed Jan's dishevelled hair behind her ear. "This explains a lot, January. This is why you didn't get angry with David when he stood you up at school, and why you've been so worried about the long hours he's been working." She took her daughter's hands in hers. "You shouldn't be going to church because you think you have to make some sort of atonement for your dad's death, or simply to keep me happy. Faith must come from the best part of your heart, the part that gives you joy and peace."

As Jan lay in her bed that night, she thought about what her mother had said, and what the priests had told her for years. Then she remembered Willow's strange and gentle faith. It took a long time for her to fall asleep.

Chapter 13

Jan woke up on Sunday envisioning how she would handle the series of S-bends on the track. Today she would find out if she had what it took. When she came down to breakfast, there was a note from her mom. *Sorry I couldn't be here to make you a big breakfast, but I'll see you at the track. Always remember — I love you, January Fournier McKenna, whatever God smiles on you, in church and out!*

Jan smiled and went to find David. He was in the study talking on the telephone. She waited, not wanting to interrupt.

"I know you were looking forward to this, Vi. I was too, but until the poaching case is solved, there's no way Corporal Sloan will give me time off, even for a delayed honeymoon." David's voice was full of regret. "If we don't get a break in the case, we'll have to cancel the trip. I'm sorry, Sweetheart."

Jan couldn't believe it! David and her mom had

planned the trip for ages. It was going to be their dream vacation, an African camera safari. It would be the first time Jan would be left home alone, a milestone in her life too. She watched as he hung up, then sat mutely staring at the phone. The desolation on his face made Jan's eyes sting with tears. It was so unfair.

She couldn't let them cancel their trip, not when she knew who the poacher was! This had to stop, and that meant telling David everything. Willow would hate her or have to forgive her, but she was going to tell David *now*.

"Go-o-o-o-d morning, David," she said as she bounced into the room. His head came up and he forced a smile. "I have a feeling you're going to get a big break in the poaching case. Willow has important new leads."

David gave her an inquiring look. "What new leads? I haven't heard anything about this."

Jan knew she was getting dangerously close to being in a corner. "Uh, I think Willow wants to talk to you about them herself. I'll go wake her and we can get this over with." It was then that she realized David was in his uniform. "I thought you had the day off for the race?"

The sadness in David's eyes deepened to regret. "I'm sorry, but I have to go in. I'll make it up, I promise." He put his hand on her shoulder. "In fact, I have a surprise for you." He walked to his credenza and picked up a box that sported bright paper and a big bow. "Your mother and I wanted to commemorate your first foray into the big leagues." He held the box out to her.

Jan remembered how Liam's dad was always buying him presents to make up for being gone, as if anything could fill the hole a missing dad left. Her fingers felt numb as she unwrapped the gift. Inside was a brand new silver Arai Corsair helmet with an elaborate feather design painted in teal and black. It was the most beautiful thing Jan had ever seen. "Wow! Oh man, this is too much! Thank you, David." She tried to smile, but she couldn't shake the look on Liam's face when he would toy with his expensive sunglasses.

"I know I haven't been able to spend as much time with you as I would have liked this last year. But, Jan, I want you to know I love you. You're the daughter of my heart and I look forward to seeing you grow and blossom into the strong, smart, courageous young woman I know is inside of you."

Jan looked into his eyes and saw the love waiting there. She ran to David and threw her arms around him. "Thank you, *Dad*." She had never called him that before, but somehow it felt natural. "I'll try never to let you down." She gave him a bear hug. "And with that in mind, I'll get Willow. We have to talk."

Running upstairs, she knocked on Willow's door, then poked her head into the room. Willow sat on the floor in the middle of her room, the sun streaming through the open window as she finished her morning prayers.

"Willow, sorry to interrupt," Jan whispered. It was foolish to whisper; she wasn't in church. She watched as Willow reverently replaced her smudge bowl in the place of honour on her dresser. It struck Jan that maybe she was in a church, one that was all around everywhere, all the time, like Willow had said.

"What's up?" Willow turned to her as Jan stepped into the room.

"We have to change our plan. We need to tell David now." Her voice seemed loud in the stillness of the sunny room.

"Jan, we have to wait."

"But Willow," Jan moved closer, her voice pleading. "David can help us find out who else is involved. You have to trust him. There are people's lives being messed with here, not to mention giving that creep more time to kill another bear."

"What are you two talking about?" David's voice from the doorway made both girls whirl around.

David and Liam stood staring at them.

Jan felt her face go red. They were so busted! "David! I didn't see you standing there."

"Obviously. Liam came to wish you luck today, and I thought I'd bring him up to surprise you, but it sounds like I'm the one who got the surprise. Now, explain what I just overheard."

Jan heard the steel edge to his tone. She looked from David to Liam and then to Willow. Willow nodded her head almost imperceptibly.

Taking a deep breath, Jan knew they were

committed now and there was no turning back. "David, you should sit down. We have something to tell you."

David sat in the dormer seat and listened while Jan and Willow explained that Dyer was the poacher. They confessed to finding details of the poaching in both Rainbow and Banff, and told how Willow had gone to Wapiti Trail Outfitters and discovered that the guide from Rainbow was now in Banff, calling himself Dyer.

David was up to speed in no time. "How can you be so sure he's the poacher? You said you had proof — how'd you get it?" All three studiously avoided his eyes.

"I supplied it," Liam spoke up. "You see, I'm kind of good at checking things out on the Internet, stuff most mere mortals couldn't get at —"

"You're a hacker," David interrupted.

"I don't like to use labels. But, I guess if it makes it clearer for you then, yes, I dabble a little. I hacked into a few restricted sites and also Dyer's e-mails. That's how we're sure he's our man." Liam's mouth was in a tense line and Jan wondered if he was worried about the consequences of confessing to an RCMP officer that he was a serious hacker. "Willow knew Dyer was the guide from Rainbow, but needed some hard proof he was into poaching. It was totally my idea to break into his e-mails to get the goods on him."

"Liam, you can't do this …" Willow began.

"It's okay, Willow. I know what I'm doing."

Liam shot her a glance that said "shut up" loud and clear.

"I helped," Jan added quickly as she moved to stand beside Liam. "We used my computer and did all the hacking from here." Jan couldn't chance the authorities impounding Liam's computer. It would kill him. "See, I thought it was Willow who was doing the poaching because of the dot maps. When I caught her snooping in your study, I had to know for sure …"

Willow's face radiated embarrassment. "I was using the handcuffs David left on the desk to practise my speed cuffing. A girl never knows when she'll need to use a skill like that. I kind of got turned around and bumped the desk with my butt. Which is when you must have heard me, Osîmimâw."

Jan noticed Willow had called her *osimimaw*, little sister, and smiled. "Another mystery solved."

David sighed in obvious exasperation, then stood and walked over to Jan's computer. "Show me."

Liam grinned and dropped his jacket onto the window seat.

"Can you remember the code to get into Dyer's e-mails?" Jan asked.

"Like my own name." Sitting at the computer, he made only a few keystrokes and they were sailing through e-space to Dyer's web mail. Seconds later, Dyer's inbox blinked open.

Liam, Jan, and Willow stared at the screen. The inbox listed "zero e-mails." He'd deleted all his correspondence!

"Oh, man. This is a Hotmail account. Once they're gone, they are *gone!*" Jan felt frustrated and angry. "Honest, David, they were here." She wasn't sure what they were going to do.

Willow looked nervous. "Liam, we need those e-mails. They document Dyer's contacts with overseas buyers for illegal bear parts and shipment details. And one of the e-mails had two attachments: *Bear Licences Names — Drawn* and *Bear Licences — Names Substituted*. We need those to nail him in the hunting licence scam. They're our only way to find out who his partner is."

"Don't panic, Cybergirl. We know they were here …" He keyed in more code. "They came through his server …" More keyboarding. "So, hopefully, somebody has them archived and hasn't done a purge yet." Suddenly the screen winked and a list of e-mails scrolled down the monitor. "Yes!" Liam crowed. "You rookies need to have a little more faith in the Wizard."

David took over the mouse and began clicking open the e-mails. "You're right. They are exactly what would be needed to put this guy away, if it weren't for the way you obtained them." He gave each of them a look that spoke volumes.

"But don't you see, David," Jan jerked her thumb at the screen. "These e-mails prove Dyer isn't in this alone, he has an accomplice."

David shook his head. "Which means my job just got harder. Those file attachments came from a secured government site."

Willow looked from Liam to Jan, then straightened slightly as she turned to David. "It also opens the door to something the rest of us have already agreed on. Dyer isn't smart enough to break into sensitive sites to get all the information he has. The only way he could have pulled this off is if his accomplice works for Alberta Fish and Wildlife, or if," she cleared her throat, "he's a cop."

"I already figured that part out." David blew out his breath. "But right now, I have to stop the shooter, and that's Dyer. I'll worry about his partner once he's safely behind bars."

He looked around the room and when he spoke, his voice was all cop. "You've done everything you can. I want you to leave it in my hands now. Do you understand — all of you?"

Kissing Jan on the forehead, he started for the door. "January, we'll discuss your withholding of critical information when I get home tonight. Go to the race and I'll let you know what happens later. And, Jan," he smiled at her, "I know you're going to kick butt today. If I can get this wrapped up in time, I'll meet you at the restaurant tonight. I'll leave my cell phone on so you can call me after the race."

Chapter 14

Willow sat on the edge of Jan's desk and looked at Liam. "I appreciate what you're trying to do, but I can't let you take the heat for this."

Liam smiled and pointed both index fingers at Willow like he held twin laser pistols. "That's where you're wrong, Cop Girl. You have to let me. I want Dyer put away, too."

Willow hesitated. "Well, okay. On one condition." Liam looked at her. "You stop with the cutesy names!"

"Gotcha, Wonder Willow." He frowned and sat up, re-reading the screen. "You know, there's something about these e-mails that's been puzzling me." He scrolled down the list and opened the e-mail. "Some of them seem personal, like Dyer knew the guy he was e-mailing. And it sounds like the other party was a local."

All three of them read the messages, but they weren't signed.

Jan's eyes went wide. "That paragraph there." She pointed to the screen. "He talks about supplies dropped at GR Campground. Read what the other guy said."

Liam read the message out loud. *"Call when you arrive Supplies dropped at Glacier Road Campground Have buyer in China Grizz."* He shrugged. "Yeah, so? The date is three months ago when Dyer first got here. The mystery partner already set up a camp for him and found a buyer in China who deals in grizzly parts."

Jan shook her head excitedly. "I don't think so. This creepoid doesn't use proper punctuation in his e-mails. Put the periods in and it reads like this: *Call when you arrive. Supplies dropped at Glacier Road Campground. Have buyer in China. Grizz.* As in *Sincerely, your partner, Grizz.*" She'd heard this name somewhere and searched her memory. Then her stomach wrenched as it hit her.

"Jan, what's going on? Who is it?" Liam's voice had an edge to it and Jan realized her panic was contagious.

She walked to her window and tried to calm down. Her squirrel buddy was sitting on the ledge, looking in at her. Jan stared into the tiny black eyes, then took a deep breath. "Willow, do you remember that first morning after you came to stay with us, and Corporal Sloan told David about the poaching at Iron Rock?"

Willow nodded.

"David called Corporal Sloan by his nickname,

Grizz! He's Grizz! Willow, Corporal Sloan is Dyer's partner." Jan tried to keep her words steady and her tone calm. "He's the inside man at the RCMP." Jan could see the skeptical look on Willow's face. "It explains how an idiot like Dyer was able to get the information on the bears and the rigged hunting licences. Corporal Sloan, with his RCMP security clearances, would make the changes, then feed the information to Dyer. Dyer would receive all the licences and could poach any bears he came across. There'd be no other hunters in the area."

Willow closed her eyes for a second. "This sucks big time. I liked the guy. He was a great partner and a good cop, up until this second. But what you say makes sense." She stood beside Jan and watched the squirrel as it shrilled a greeting. "I told you that your spirit helper would be here when you needed him."

Jan's brow furrowed. "What spirit helper? This thing's been a team effort with you as our leader. You were onto Dyer, and knew he had a partner. Liam and I just helped you fill in the blanks."

Willow came as close to blushing as Jan had ever seen. "Yeah, I guess I was pretty cool, huh? You know a girl could come to like this police stuff. It feels good to get the bad guy."

"Exactly!" Jan agreed. "Hey! Catching Dyer and Sloan will really help when you join the RCMP. Busting up a poaching ring while still a Supernumerary Summer Student will look sweet on your application."

Willow held up her hand to stop Jan. "Don't get any ideas. I'm here to catch Dyer. I'm going back to complete my schooling and then I have to finish becoming a healer. I only joined the RCMP Summer Student Program so I could take this guy down."

For the first time, Jan thought she heard regret in Willow's voice. "But maybe you weren't meant to be a healer. Maybe you can help your people more by becoming a law enforcement officer. Don't you think your grandfather would have wanted you to be happy before anything else?"

Willow looked resigned. "I have to walk the path chosen for me."

Jan shook her head. "That's not the way I see it. I've learned enough about the old ways to know you should walk the true path that is right for you. Didn't you say to listen to both your heart and spirit helper to find that path?"

Willow slowly nodded. "Maybe we have to be willing to make course changes. Some paths aren't on the map, but it doesn't mean one of them might not be the right path after all." Then her face broke into a wide smile. "And who knows, I might get posted back here and can bust you for pushing that bike of yours until you're melting the yellow dots off the road."

"You'd have to catch me first!" Jan giggled, then reached out a finger and tapped the glass where the squirrel was sitting. "And as far as spirit guides … You're going to tell me this little guy is mine?" She nodded at the squirrel. "I thought they were ghosts or scary things that flew around on dark nights and said, Boo! This little guy doesn't look very spooky to me." She remembered all the squirrels she had noticed in the last few weeks. This couldn't be the same one, but she couldn't prove it wasn't. One squirrel looks pretty much like another except … She looked at the notch in the squirrel's ear. No, it wasn't possible. A tingle ran down Jan's spine.

Willow sighed. "Another of those unexpected paths."

Jan looked at Willow. "About the Creator and my spirit guide and all that stuff — you really, truly believe and you made me see there is so much in the world we don't understand. You showed me that faith comes in all shapes, sizes, and colours. *Meegwetch*, Willow, thank you."

Willow gave a tiny nod of her head. "Many paths, one destination, Jan. But now, with Sloan involved, this case is about to become a block-buster. I believe it's a Canadian tradition that the Mounties always get their man. Well, in this case it's the Supernumerary Summer Student who's about to do the deed, but I guess I'm close enough to the real thing."

Willow gave Jan a quick hug. "Knock 'em dead today, kid."

She left and Jan watched her climb aboard her rocket. Willow looked up at Jan and waved, started her bike, and disappeared to begin a whole new page in her life.

Jan turned and found Liam standing behind her with a bedraggled bouquet of daisies clutched in his hand. "I guess I shouldn't have tossed my coat on these. I came here to wish you good luck with the race." He thrust the flowers at her. "Good luck."

Jan noticed some of them still had roots attached and wondered whose garden had donated the happy handful. The flowers were way past droopy, verging on terminal. She suspected they were the wild variety of daisy that grew in the meadows around Banff; wildflowers didn't like to be picked. "Thanks." They stood silently looking at each other, until Jan finally cleared her throat. "I'd better get these in water."

They went downstairs to the kitchen where Jan found an old pickle jar to hold her first bouquet of flowers. They did look kind of nice, even if they were wilted beyond recognition.

Liam looked at his watch. "Hadn't you better get going?" Jan looked at him blankly. "The race …"

She looked at the kitchen clock. She should have been gone two hours ago. "Oh, man, Grey is going to kill me."

Jan ran to get her leather jacket, riding boots, and gloves, then they trooped out to the driveway. Liam held her battered helmet as she zipped up her jacket. Taking the helmet, she pulled it down over her head and flipped the visor up as she fastened the chin strap. "I'll call you later and let you know how it goes."

Liam smiled shyly. He leaned forward and kissed

her on the tip of her nose, which was all he could get to with her helmet on. "Go get 'em, Jan."

Jan was so surprised she could only nod. "Will you tell me something?" she asked in a breathy whisper.

His voice was low and intimate. "Sure. For you, anything."

"What does the *B* in B. Liam Simpson stand for?"

His eyes squinched shut and he groaned. "Okay, you asked for it." He took a deep breath. "Bartholomew."

She frowned. "Bartholomew? What's wrong with that? It's a little old-fashioned, but you could always shorten it to …" Then she clued in. "Oh."

"Going through life being known as Bart Simpson is not something I want to even think about. So that tidbit of information stays between you and me. Deal?"

She smiled and nodded. "Deal. I think Liam suits you way more anyway." She hit her helmet with her palm. "Yikes! I nearly forgot!" A twinkle lit up her eyes. "Wait here a minute." She ran back into the house and came out with her new shiny helmet cradled in her arms. "For weeks now, I've been playing in your cyber-universe. Don't get me wrong, it's been a blast. But if we're going to take our relationship to a new level, you need to spend a little time in my world. Put this on." She thrust her new helmet at him. "We've got a race to win."

Epilogue

As they sped down the Trans-Canada highway towards Calgary, Jan felt Liam's arms around her waist and his body pressed snugly up against hers. She could get used to this in a big hurry.

They arrived at the track minutes before the start of the final race. When they made it to where Grey had pitted, Jan was surprised to see her older brother trying to struggle into her racing leathers.

She watched him unsuccessfully wriggling for a few seconds. Then she said, "You'll never get them zipped up over that bannock paunch of yours, Grey!"

"Jan!" Grey's head jerked up in surprise, then his face flashed through a series of emotions — worry, anger, and finally relief. "Where have you been? Why didn't you call? After you missed qualifying, I thought something grim had happened. I tried to phone David, but no one at the detachment would tell me anything."

Jan and Liam looked at each other and grinned.

"Oh, I think David's a little busy right now." Jan giggled. "And so is Willow and Todd Dyer. And I bet Corporal Sloan has his hands full too."

At that moment, Jan's mom emerged from the back of their trailer. "I'm not sure what you're talking about, but it sounds as though we're going to need a family discussion after this race is over. Liam, I didn't expect to see you here today, dear."

Liam pulled off his borrowed helmet and handed it to Jan. "I couldn't let my girlfriend ride in her big race without being here to see her win."

Jan blushed. "All I have to say is, these second-place crotch-rocket jockeys are in for a surprise today!"

Grey finished wiggling out of the racing leathers and tossed them to Jan. "Girlfriend, eh? Can you tear yourself away from lover boy here long enough to get suited up?"

"What did the officials say when I missed qualifying?"

Grey shrugged. "I told them we were still in, but you'd been held up. I had to tell them you'd be happy to start from the back of the grid. There's a field of twelve that you'll have to get past."

Jan knew her job had just become twelve times harder. "Why were you trying to shoehorn your body into my riding leathers?"

"Because, my better-late-than-never-Sister, I was going to ride for you." He waggled his wrist up and down. "It's stiff, but I was hoping it would loosen up by turn two."

163

Jan laughed. "You are a desperate man, Grey. And I promise never to do this to you again. If I can help it," she added as she headed for the trailer to change.

* * *

Thanks to a great launch, Jan flew past the first six competitors in the field before the first turn. After that, she slowly reeled in the leaders, picking them off one by one. Her Yamaha felt like it was ready to fly, all she had to do was point it in the right direction and the bike would do the rest.

Jan's mind flashed over Willow's shaman rites and spirit helpers, then her mom's faith in her rosary and prayer. She couldn't bring herself to call on either to help her win this race. In her heart, she knew who would ultimately be her strongest help right now — January Fournier McKenna.

As she closed on the leader, Jan knew the rider was cagey and a super competitor. Mr. Suzuki and his GSX-R600 were a dynamite team. Jan stayed in his draft on the straight, edging closer to the inside of the track. The Gixxer's pilot edged over, effectively blocking her from taking an inside line on the corner.

Jan blasted into the next turn, content to stay put. On the next lap, she again edged toward the inside of the track, only to have Mr. S. move over to block her.

With one lap left, Jan knew she had to make her move. She grinned. She again blasted down the straight; boldly moving to the inside and edging closer than she had previously. Predictably, Mr. Suzuki moved down to stop her, putting himself off line for the upcoming corner. As they approached the braking zone, she waited until the last possible second, then darted wide and blasted past him on the outside. It was a gutsy move that had the fans on their feet cheering.

As she came out of the right-hander, she could see the starter waiting up ahead in his stand. Her heart started to soar. *"Yes! Yes! Yes!"* she yelled into her helmet. In his hand was the sweetest sight Jan had ever seen — a large black-and-white checkered flag.